HER SPANISH BOSS

BY

BARBARA McMAHON

To Los Sueños, Luis, Mario, Juan, Julian and Rooney.
I loved your music, you all were the best! *Viva España!*

All the characters in this book have no existence outside the imagination of the author, and have no relation whatsoever to anyone bearing the same name or names. They are not even distantly inspired by any individual known or unknown to the author, and all the incidents are pure invention.

First published in Great Britain 2004
Large Print edition 2004
Harlequin Mills & Boon Limited,
Eton House, 18-24 Paradise Road,
Richmond, Surrey TW9 1SR

ISBN 0 263 18129 4

Set in Times Roman 16½ on 18 pt.
16-1204-48976

Printed and bound in Great Britain
by Antony Rowe Ltd, Chippenham, Wiltshire

CHAPTER ONE

RACHEL GOODSON counted the Euros once more. The total hadn't changed. She was 470 Euros away from destitution. Or the use of her bank card which she refused to do. To use it would give away her location. She hadn't come all the way to this little Spanish town to be found so easily by her powerful father. She had meant her final statement. She was leaving home, leaving him and his outrageous demands and his unbelievable betrayal.

She was also leaving behind the man her father had hand picked to marry her. This was the twenty-first century, not feudal times. She would pick out her own husband, thank you very much. And it would not be someone who had more in common with her father than with her. Anger churned when she thought about recent events.

She took a deep breath, sipped her lemonade and gazed at the fishing boats bobbing along the weathered wooden dock. A couple of old men mended nets. The hot sunshine didn't seem to bother them. She would have sought shade.

Her small suitcase rested at her side. Her voluminous purse held all the important items, such as passport, money and credit cards—which she also refused to use. Her father would know as soon as he received the bills where she was if she charged a single thing. For her rebellion to be successful, she had to stay hidden from the powerful men who sought her.

Rachel's rebellion, she thought wryly. Could she pull it off? She had done her best to vanish two weeks ago. So far she had managed beautifully on her own. But her money was running out.

The white buildings behind her reflected the afternoon sun, gleaming in the brilliant light. She'd fallen in love with the little village perched on the edge of the Mediterranean Sea the moment she'd stepped off the bus a short time before. She had already been charmed by the friendly people. Now she delighted in the simple beauty of the setting. And most important, she felt safe with the isolation. This place didn't have the glamour of Madrid, nor the appeal of Majorca. The beach curving around the bay was practically desolate. Definitely not the place her father would think of for his only child.

The hills that rose behind seemed to shelter the town from the rest of the country. To the left, olive groves marched into the distance, their rows neat and symmetrical. To the right the ground was untamed, a tangle of trees, bushes and wild flowers. At the top, almost like a crown, sat a grey stone *castillo.*

She had not seen any sign indicating a *parador* nearby, which meant it was privately owned. Too bad, she'd love to spend one night in a castle in Spain.

Her financial situation, however, was more pressing. She needed to see if she could find work. It was unlikely without proper papers, but there had to be someone willing to let her earn some money without the formality of work permits. Maybe a local restaurant needed a waitress, with no questions asked. Or— Or what?

She had never held a paying job. Her experiences had been geared to planning lavish charity events or sharing hosting duties with her father at high-powered business dinners. Since graduating from college several years earlier, she had dabbled with establishing a career, only to be talked out of it again and again by her father. He needed her too much, he'd said. No one else could handle the social aspects of his business as well as she did. If her mother had lived, she could have handled all that.

Anger threatened again at the lies and deception. Her mother had lived. Two weeks ago Rachel had learned the truth. She gripped her glass tightly, wishing she had said even more to the man who had directed her every move until she'd learned of his deception.

He had the gall to expect her to marry Paul Cambrick. An alliance for business gain. No amount of arguments from Rachel had swayed him from his position. The pressure had grown intolerable.

Running away probably wasn't the smartest thing she'd ever done, but she was sure it made an impression on her father. Now she needed to find work to prove she didn't need her father or Paul to live on. She definitely was not going to marry Paul no matter what. If she never saw Paul Cambrick again, it might be too soon. Pompous ass. And threats to cut off her trust fund would be fruitless once she was earning a living.

She gazed at the sparkling water, trying to let her anger ebb. Of course independence had sounded perfect in her bedroom in Malibu. She remembered pacing back and forth, coming up with one idea after another. In retrospect, it would have been far easier to disappear in the States. She could have found work anywhere. Coming to Spain had been impulsive, giving into a long-held dream—and the determination to put as much distance between herself and her father.

"Can I get you anything else?" the young waiter asked in rapid Spanish.

"No, thank you. This is fine," she replied, a bit more slowly. He'd been more than friendly since she'd chosen the small table near the edge of the patio. And patient with her California version of Spanish. She could be understood, and understand him, but only if the pace was slow. She had to ask repeatedly for others to slow down since her arrival in Spain.

"*Americano?*" he asked with a wide grin.

"*Si.*" She wished it wasn't so obvious. Glancing around at all the dark-haired women sitting at other tables at the café, Rachel knew her blond hair stuck out like a beacon. But she could have been German or Dutch, why did he immediately peg her as American?

"Oh, are you here for Señor Alvares's job?" the young man asked excitedly. "We have been wondering when another secretary would arrive. If not soon, Maria will recover and return."

She blinked, wondering if she'd understood the rapid Spanish correctly. "Where is Señor Alvares?" Could it be this man wanted an American secretary? No way, her luck couldn't be running that good.

He pointed to the *castillo* on the hillside. The harsh grey granite seemed indomitable, rising loftily above the trees and shrubs that partially hid it from the town.

She looked at it, various scenarios flashing in her mind. Maybe she couldn't spend the night at the *castillo*, but could she spend a few days there? What kind of secretary did the man need? She didn't have a formal background in secretarial work in English, much less Spanish. And she was having a bit of trouble conversing in Spanish, but once she'd been here a little longer, she was sure she'd pick up the different nuances. Still, she had a lot of organizing experience. Could deal with difficult vendors, meet deadlines. How hard could the work be?

''How does one get to the *castillo*?'' she asked, already determined to give it a try. Answer the phone, make appointments, do some typing, she could handle it all. The worst he could say would be no. If luck was on her side, maybe she could get a temporary job to tide her over until she figured out her next step.

* * *

Twenty minutes later Rachel was flying up the mountainous road in an old cab that probably had been in service before she was born. The driver looked old enough to have invented cars. He drove with abandon, gesturing to sights as they rounded one hairpin turn after another. The view grew more spectacular the higher they went. Not that Rachel could focus on the view—she was holding on for dear life.

Luck was definitely with her on the ride, she thought, trying to keep from sliding from side to side on the worn vinyl seat. They hadn't crashed headfirst into another vehicle. There were none descending. They hadn't flown off the edge of the road, either, though it was touch and go a couple of times.

At one bad turn, the driver crossed himself, falling silent for a moment. Rachel wondered if she should be frightened—rather more frightened than taking her life in her hands by getting into this cab in the first place. But before she could decide, they rounded another turn and he began his rapid spiel again.

She caught most of what he was saying, expounding on the beauties of the town, the wonders of Spain and old glories. Was he practicing to be a tour guide?

They rounded another bend and Rachel gasped at the magnificence of the stone castle before her. It was not huge, but large enough to be impressive. It was in excellent repair. The grounds were simple, green and lush, but without the ornamental formality she had seen in other *castillos*. There was no one in sight, nor any cars. Was anyone home? She hadn't even considered that in her impetuous decision.

The cab stopped before the steps leading to the ornately carved double front doors. The driver turned and grinned at her, holding out his hand.

She paid him, grabbed her bag and slid across the seat. Still staring at the granite edifice, she heard the cab drive away. She had debated having him wait while she asked for an interview, but decided she'd be in a stronger position to get that interview if she had no means of return readily available. Señor Alvares would have to interview her if only to fill the time until a taxi could be summoned.

If he were home.

Why hadn't she thought of that before?

What if no one was here? She'd not be able to use a phone, which would mean a long hike back to the café if that was the case.

''Positive thinking, that's the key,'' she murmured, mounting the steps and ringing the bell to the right of the doors.

Endless moments slipped by.

Rachel was conscious of birds twittering in nearby trees. The soft soughing of the wind through the branches was pleasant. The late afternoon heat was starting to get to her, however, despite the breeze. She turned and looked at the view of the Mediterranean spread out before her as far as she could see. Awe-inspiring. The spanking white buildings of the village contrasted with the blue at the edge of the sea. There was a quiet kind of hush around the castle. For a moment she thought of Heathcliff and the moors. A brooding silence seemed to pervade the grounds despite the bright sunshine and birdsong.

She tried the bell again.

A moment later the left door was opened.

"*Si?*" A woman with a kerchief over her head and a duster in one hand looked at her.

"*Señor Alvares, por favor,*" Rachel said, glad her voice wasn't quaking like her knees. She hoped there was a job and she could get it. Bluff your way through, she told herself, raising her chin.

"*Uno momento.*" The woman shut the door.

Astonished, Rachel stared at the dark wood. How rude!

She leaned on the bell again.

It was flung open a moment later. A tall man gazed down at her, his frown intimidating. Rachel stared back. Tall, dark and dangerous was her first thought. He was easily six inches over her own five feet seven inches. His dark hair brushed the top of his collar. His dark eyes were narrowed as he assessed her. His face was planes and angles, with not a spark of warmth anywhere. His size and demeanor would be enough to scare anyone off.

Except someone in desperate straights who needed a job.

"Señor Alvares?" she asked brightly.

"Whatever it is you are selling, we don't want it. Leave or I'll call the *guardia*," he growled, moving to shut the door a second time.

Rachel stepped forward and pushed against it, obviously taking him by surprise. She quickly sidestepped into the entry foyer and swallowed. Tenacity was one of her strong points. Her father usually called it stubbornness.

"I've come to see Señor Alvares. If you are not he, please let him know I'm here," she said arrogantly. She had no idea who this man was, but being assertive might be the only way she could get an interview. She wanted the job more and more, if only to prove she could get it.

"Who are you?" he asked, his stance more rigid. "And what are you doing here?"

"Rachel Goodson. I'm here about the secretary's job."

"I have a secretary," he said bluntly.

She looked at him in surprise. "Señor Alvares? How do you do? I heard in the village you needed a new secretary. An American secretary. I'd be perfect for the job.''

He pushed the door shut. Instantly Rachel wished he had not. She was alone with this stranger, in a remote location. Where had the maid gone? No one else really knew she was here. Would the cab driver even remember bringing her here after a day or two? Would the maid known she'd come into the house?

''Don't believe all you hear in the village. The people there tend to gossip,'' he said, crossing his arms across his chest and staring at her.

Heathcliff, she thought again. Dark and brooding. He wore a blue silk shirt, open at the neck, and dark trousers. Maybe he should wear all black, she thought frivolously. Dragging her fanciful thoughts back to reality, she frowned at his remark.

''So you are not looking for a temporary secretary?'' she said, disappointed. She had hoped to find an easy solution to her own dilemma. She should have known better.

''Are you really a secretary, or a reporter who heard I needed help and pounced on the chance for an exclusive?'' he asked suspiciously.

''Exclusive what?''

He raised an eyebrow as if in disbelief. ''Exclusive interview, of course.''

''Are you newsworthy?'' she asked.

''American?'' he asked suddenly.

''From California,'' she said. ''But I speak Spanish as you can see, and I'm even better at reading and writing it.'' She hoped he didn't question her experience in the secretarial field too closely. Though planning events and serving on various charity boards would surely constitute experience of a kind.

''How's your English grammar?'' he asked in that language.

''Perfect,'' she replied in the same, showing some surprise. ''You speak English?''

''As you can see,'' he said impatiently.

She waited, hoping he'd expand on that brusque statement, but he said nothing. The few words he'd spoken, however, had been unaccented. As if American English was his native tongue. Rachel wondered how long the silence would stretch out. She refused to be the first to break it. She was tired of being pushed around by dominant males in her life. From now on, she would not be intimidated by anyone. If Señor Alvares wanted her to leave, he could call her a cab!

Reluctantly she had to admit maybe she'd been too quick to jump on a faint job possibility. If he didn't have a position, he didn't have one. Dashing up here on the say so of a young waiter had really been dumb. What about work permits, secretarial references? Just because she desperately wanted a means to earn enough to tide her over until she decided what to do didn't mean this man wanted to hire her.

He looked at her small suitcase sitting on the black-and-white tiled floor beside her.

"You came prepared to start today?" he asked.

"Yes." No good carrying on a bluff if you didn't go full out, she decided. She angled up her chin slightly. "I'm ready to start immediately."

For a moment she thought a hint of amusement showed in his dark eyes, but decided it had to be a trick of the faint light spilling in from the fanned windows over the double doors. He didn't look as if anything amused him.

She longed to look around, to see what the rest of the *castillo* looked like. It might be her only chance to be inside a castle in Spain, but she maintained eye contact. A glimmer of hope blossomed. If he asked about her staying, maybe he was seriously thinking about hiring her.

"Come with me," he said, turning abruptly and heading down the corridor.

She picked up her bag and followed, hurrying so she didn't lose sight of him as he took long strides down the dim hallway.

He entered a room to the right and Rachel quickly followed, stopping at the door and staring in surprise. The sheer size caught her attention first, easily the size of two or three rooms at home. They were brightly lit from the floor-to-ceiling windows that overlooked the sea. A set of French doors stood open, letting in the fragrant air.

There were two large desks, both covered in papers, files and books. A computer desk sat near one, every other flat surface, including the keyboard, overflowing with papers.

"If you can read my writing and transcribe the work, maybe we'll see about your staying until Maria returns," he murmured in Spanish.

She looked at Señor Alvares and smiled brightly. "I'm sure I can manage, if you'd tell me which desk is mine."

He looked at her. "Let's get some things clear first. Everything you see or learn here is confidential, do you understand? Any hint of a breach, of betrayal, and I'll make you sorry you were born!"

Rachel blinked, swallowing hard and wondering if other secretaries got threats as part of the job interview. If so, either they were more intrepid than she had ever given them credit for, or jobs must be so tough to get they put up with anything!

"Agreed." She only hoped the position paid enough that she didn't have to stay long. She was already regretting her impulsive visit. Maybe she should return to the village and forget the entire thing. Only the thought of having to use her credit cards and alert her father stopped her.

"How did you learn of the job opening? You aren't from the agency," he said, his arms crossed over his chest, feet spread.

Rachel didn't wish to tell him she'd heard about it from a waiter, yet how else? "A friend told me," she replied vaguely.

"Let me see your passport." He held out his hand.

She rummaged in her purse. Holding it out, she watched as he studied it. Folding it shut, he slipped it into his pocket.

"Hey, I need that."

"Not if you are working here."

"I can't go anywhere without it in this country," she protested.

"The job comes with room and board. You'll get it back when I'm assured you aren't some tabloid reporter."

"I told you I wasn't!"

"My secretary broke her arm in three places while hiking and won't be able to return to work for a few more weeks. If you suit, you can stay until she returns,'' he said in English.

Glancing at her suitcase, he continued. ''Maria has her own apartments in the left wing, but she is convalescing with her mother in Madrid. Her rooms are not available, but you can certainly find another bedroom upstairs somewhere. There are twenty-seven bedrooms and I only use one.'' He strode over to the larger of the desks and picked up a stack of yellow paper.

''This is where you start. You do know word processing, I trust?''

''Señor,'' Rachel began.

''Call me Luis. You'll have to find your own dinner today. My housekeeper, Esperenza, is on holiday and Ana doesn't cook. In fact, she'll be leaving at four. But Esperenza returns tomorrow, *gracias a Dios* and meals will be provided. If you can't find the file Maria started, begin another. Formatting is double-spaced, one inch margins all round. Any questions?''

Rachel had a thousand, but the impatience with which he regarded her had her hold her tongue. She had a job and a place to stay. Her immediate needs had been met. How hard could it be to transcribe those pages, whatever they were?

When she shook her head to indicate she had no questions, he nodded once and turned to leave through the French doors.

Rachel remained where she was. It was the most bizarre interview she'd ever heard of. And no mention of salary.

Still, with room and board, her 470 Euros would stretch out a long time. Easily covering the respite she'd find here until Maria returned, she thought. Maybe by then she would have recovered enough from her shock of discovery to decide what to do.

In the meantime, she was in Spain! She'd had a love affair with the country since she'd first started studying Spanish in high school. Collecting posters, brochures, photographs and books for years, she was thrilled to be here.

The last two weeks had been wonderful. She'd been to the Prado, toured the royal palace in Madrid. She'd sipped café con leche at sidewalk cafés and wandered old narrow streets with venerable buildings that enchanted. She couldn't wait to explore more on her days off. There was so much history in the country, she'd forever be learning something new. There were the fabulous gardens and old cities which she couldn't wait to see. She wanted to visit Valencia, Barcelona, Seville. There were a hundred things she could do on her free days.

Work first, she admonished herself. She'd make herself so indispensable he'd have to keep her on until Maria recovered. From the looks of things, he'd need someone just to keep track of the paper. Who had time to answer phones, arrange appointments and deal with the mail?

He hadn't made any mention of routine. What did he do?

She frowned. How effective a secretary would she be without that basic knowledge?

She crossed the room and peered out onto the terrace. Luis Alvares had disappeared. It looked as if she needn't worry about him hovering over her while she stumbled through the first awkward moments of a new job.

First things first, however. Rachel took her suitcase and headed for the hallway. She retraced her way to the front foyer and climbed the wide stairs. Looking left and right when she reached the second floor, she hesitated. If Maria had quarters in the left wing, maybe she should find a room there as well. As she walked along the carpeted corridor, she studied the paintings on the walls. Dark and depressing for the most part. Were they portraits of ancestors?

She stopped by the first door on her left and knocked. Feeling silly when she knew she was virtually alone in the house, she opened it and peeped inside.

Drapes were closed. Through the dim light, she could see a huge four poster bed and heavy ornately carved furnishings. The room itself was as large as the biggest room in her father's house.

In only moments, Rachel had opened the drapes and the windows to allow sunshine and fresh air in. The view was the same as from the front door, without any shrubs or trees to block it. Near the shore the Mediterranean was a light turquoise, but farther out the water turned a deep indigo. On the horizon, she saw a huge ship.

"Señorita, Señor Alvares told me to find you. I have come to make the bed," the maid said from the doorway, a pile of sheets in her arms.

"Oh, thank you. If you leave the sheets, I can manage."

"Oh, no." The woman looked shocked.

Rachel shrugged and started to unpack while Ana made the bed.

After freshening up, Rachel headed back to the office.

Curious about her new employer, she was disappointed to see the room remained empty. Where had he gone? For someone who didn't trust she wasn't a reporter, he'd sure disappeared fast. What was to stop her from snooping into everything?

She crossed to the desk and looked at the papers, startled to find them written in English. Quickly scanning one or two, she realized she was reading a manuscript. He was a writer.

But why write in English? Why not Spanish?

She studied the page numbers, searching out from different piles, putting the sheets in numeric order, noting the lowest page she could find was page seventy-three. Where were the first seventy-two pages? Maybe on the other desk.

Rachel looked in vain for the first pages. But as she ruffled through the pages, she noticing other papers apparently dealing with the olive industry. There were trade publications, reports and a reference to cargo containers.

"Was there something I can help you with, or shall I leave you to snoop to your heart's content?"

She spun around. Luis stood in the open doorway, watching her with an intensity that was intimidating.

"I couldn't find the first pages. It's a book, isn't it? But it starts on page seventy-three."

"Maria transcribed the first part before she injured herself. I said to start a new file if you couldn't find hers."

"Oh." Rachel felt as if she'd made a fool of herself. She was only trying to be organized.

"Then I'll look for it on the computer," she said with as much dignity as she could muster.

She tried to stack the pile of papers neatly, but fumbled as she grew more and more nervous with his steady regard. She wasn't here to steal the family silver, for heaven's sake. Couldn't he back off?

She looked up, but he hadn't moved. "Um, you didn't tell me about answering the phone or opening any mail."

"The mail can wait until you catch up on the typing. I've been taking it into the office in Benidorm. They can continue to handle it there. The phone won't often ring. If I'm here, I'll answer it. If not, take a message."

"Will you be gone often?"

His eyes narrowed at her question. "Why?"

"So I'll know how much time I'll need for the phones."

"I work in Benidorm."

"You write there?"

"I said I work there. Writing is a hobby. I do it as time allows."

She looked at the thick stack of sheets to be transcribed. He must have a lot of time.

''What do you do?'' she asked.

''For someone who claims she isn't a reporter, you have a lot of questions.''

''Forget it, then. I have work to do.''

''It's after five. You can wait until the morning to start.''

''So you don't expect me to slave night and day,'' she murmured.

''When you are ready for dinner, you can help yourself.'' He ignored her comment, but the lift of one eyebrow suggested he heard her.

''I don't know where the kitchen is.''

''It's down the right corridor at the end of the main hall.''

She placed the manuscript pages she had straightened on the desk by the computer. She couldn't wait to get started to see if the book was anything she'd like to read.

''How long have you been writing?'' she asked.

''Another question?''

''Don't you expect a secretary to take an interest in her boss's business? Maybe if you'd give a little information, I wouldn't have to ask so much. Is your other job raising olives or something?'' She held up a thick report by someone named Juan.

''Raising olives?''

Once again Rachel thought she caught a glimpse of amusement in his eyes.

''Growing olives? Whatever.''

''I am in charge of the Alvares Olive Consortium. It has been in the Alvares family for four generations. And yes, I guess you could say we grow olives. We also process them, making the finest oil as well as producing a line of Spanish olives for the American market.''

''So in your copious spare time you write? Isn't running a business enough?''

He inclined his head slightly. ''I enjoy writing.''

''English Literature was my major in college. I'm surprised to find you writing in English, however. I would have thought you'd write in your native language.'' While not another question, she sure wished he would explain.

"English is my native language, as well as Spanish. My mother is an American."

"She is?" She couldn't think of anything else to say without asking another question. How had his parents met? Were they still living? Did he have books published in the United States? Should she recognize his name? Vainly she tried to recall any books by a Luis Alvares. Nothing came to mind. Not that she knew the name of every author published in the U.S.

Finally she moved toward the door. She'd see what she could get for dinner. It was early, but she'd been traveling most of the day and was tired. Leaving felt like escape. She wanted some time to herself. Dealing with this man was difficult enough. Tomorrow she'd be rested and raring to go.

Passing Luis, she could smell the faint tang of his aftershave, feel some of the warmth from his body. She'd noticed Spaniards didn't require the same amount of personal space she was used to. They stood closer, almost touching, while talking with friends. Stepping away, she hoped she didn't look like she felt intimidated.

He surprised her by leading the way down the hall and into the kitchen. It was huge. Rachel could imagine it staffed with a dozen people, all scurrying to fix a meal for the imperial master of the castle. Though modern equipment was in place, the huge room reflected its early days. Had the castle ever defended its land against invaders? Or fallen to enemy hands?

She wished she felt comfortable enough to ask. The building was old enough to have been through the two world wars, and a lot more.

"Do you cook?" Luis asked.

"Yes. Shall I make dinner?"

"Take anything from the cupboards and refrigerator you wish. Esperenza left me several meals to heat in the microwave. If you wish to have one of them, help yourself." Without another word, he left.

Was Luis Alvares always so abrupt? She wasn't a guest, she reminded herself. Maybe that was his technique with employees.

Or with young women who might make a play for the lord of the manor, she thought. He seemed highly suspicious—yet had left her alone in the study. She didn't know what to think about the man, but speculation was better than dwelling on her father and his perfidy. Or Paul and his outrageous plans that never included her input.

Not that Luis Alvares was in any danger from her developing a crush. The last thing she wanted was to get involved with anyone. She had to make plans first to convince Paul she was serious in calling off their supposed alliance. He and his father seemed deaf when she'd denied there was an engagement.

Then she had to decide what to do about her mother. Would she search for her or not? How else would she discover what had really happened twenty-four years ago? Was there someone who had known her parents then who would tell her? None of her father's friends, of that she was sure. Someone else?

She was fed up with domineering men. If she ever let herself fall in love some day in the future, it would be with a man who was kind and gentle and who cherished her for herself, not one who saw her as a dynastic means to build his empire. A man to whom money wasn't important, or power. Only the happiness from living with her and a family they might start.

"But that's ages away," she said aloud. "After I find the mother I never knew was alive."

CHAPTER TWO

LUIS HEADED BACK to the study. He wasn't certain he'd done the right thing by impetuously hiring a stranger. But the fact was he needed to get the manuscript transcribed. He had a deadline looming and would rather have it typed where he could keep an eye on the progress than ship it off to New York and have someone transcribe it there.

He ought to check references. Make sure she wasn't some tabloid reporter worming herself into his household. But it was time his luck turned. He hoped she was just as she looked—a tourist who wanted to stay longer so applied for a temporary job. An American would be familiar with the slang and spelling of the words. He'd hoped she would be able to decipher his handwriting. Maria was used to it, though she complained mightily some days when he was in a hurry and rushed through the writing, or the car ride had been bumpy. If he didn't have his car and driver, he would never get as much done as he did.

He looked at the desk Rachel had been searching when he entered the office and hoped the need for secretarial support hadn't outweighed his good sense. He should find out more about the woman who had invaded his home. At least with her passport in hand, he could keep some control.

Transcription was getting too far behind to ignore. If she could handle the task, it would suffice until Maria returned. It was that or get someone in from the office. While one or two of the staff members spoke English, their mastery wasn't enough to make sure he'd used correct tense, or to catch spelling errors.

He'd talk to Esperenza when she returned in the morning, to make sure she kept an eye on Rachel. No sneaking around the place. And he'd make sure all the work-related documents were returned to Benidorm.

He'd also warn his housekeeper to refrain from talking out of turn. Having known him since he was a baby, she thought of herself more like a mother than a housekeeper. She often regaled visitors with boyhood exploits best forgotten. Of the summers he'd spent at the *castillo,* and the letters he'd so often written her when he was with his mother in America.

She was proud of him. Had been even before his literary success. His expression softened for an instant when he thought about the older woman. He loved her. She was one of only a few people on the planet he could say that about.

With Maria's accident, he was behind schedule. Maybe with Rachel he could get caught up. If not, he'd have to ship it as it was to his editor and have him get it typed. He doubted his editor would complain. The last book had been five weeks on the New York Times bestseller list, and was already in its fifth reprinting cycle. But Luis would rather have the control over the manuscript until he'd reread every page and knew it was as he wanted it.

He had other business to attend to. He often thought he would write full time if he could, but he had responsibilities for the Alvares

Olive Consortium. Tomorrow, he had a meeting with a company interested in becoming a new outlet for their extra vigin oil.

He hoped Rachel would make a dent on the handwritten manuscript pages while he was gone, and not end up spending the day searching his private records.

For the first time in three years, his curiosity rose. How had she really heard of his need for a secretary? She had said only a friend. Who? Why was she looking for a job in a remote village like this one? Vacationing and running out of funds before she was ready to return home, he suspected. If her story was true and she wasn't a reporter.

Luis's interest was piqued. He liked a good mystery—whether one he devised or one that fell into his lap. Who was Rachel Goodson and why was she here?

If she were a reporter, she was doing a great job of hiding the fact. Unless she was too clever to show her hand the first day. Yet, he'd swear she had been genuinely perplexed when he'd accused her of seeking a story. Was it possible there were people on the earth who didn't know of the great love of Luis and Bonita? And the tragic end?

Cynically, he doubted it. More likely she was playing some deep game. He'd watch her. If there was any sign of betrayal, he'd make sure she rued the day. He'd learned his lesson with women. A healthy dose of cynicism kept things on an even keel. One mistake could be excused to anyone. A second would be downright foolish.

Rachel made herself an omelet and ate at the large kitchen table. Fresh fruit finished her makeshift meal and once she was done, she washed the dishes. No sense in his housekeeper arriving to a messy kitchen when she had nothing else to do to while away the evening.

Next she'd take a walk around the *castillo* and then retire. Though what she'd do for the hours after that until bedtime, she hadn't a clue. The book she'd bought at the bus depot yesterday was almost as boring as reading a telephone directory. Maybe Luis had a book lying around that he'd written. Might as well learn a bit more about her elusive employer.

She returned to the study. Luis was sitting at the desk near the doors, his chair turned, staring out into the early evening. He looked over his shoulder when he heard her. His dark eyes watchful.

Rachel glanced at the stack of papers on the desk. Were they the manuscript pages she'd put in order? Had he been checking them? Probably in order to gauge how much she got done tomorrow.

For some reason, she was uneasy about entering the study with him there. If felt almost as if she were trespassing.

"Did you want something?" he asked, turning and standing.

"I thought if you had already published a book, I could read that this evening," she said. His gaze unnerved her, as if he were trying to see down to her very soul. His watchfulness annoyed her. If he couldn't trust her, he shouldn't have hired her.

No, he thought she was a reporter. Why would a reporter try to infiltrate her way into this man's house? She'd seen nothing out of the ordinary today. Except Luis Alvares himself. He was definitely not an ordinary man.

"I have published several as it happens." He crossed to a cabinet on the side wall. The wooden doors were shut. When he opened them, they revealed several shelves of books. He selected one and handed it to Rachel.

She looked at it, and then at him.

"You're J. L. Allan?"

He waited.

"I've read your books. All of them, I think. I love mysteries." She studied a familiar cover, a smile breaking out. "Wow, I'm going to see the next one before it gets published!"

Still he waited.

She looked up, puzzlement causing her smile to fade. "This is what you meant by confidential, isn't it? So no one knows about the new book before it hits the bookstores? I would never tell a soul. You can trust me."

She didn't like his skeptical expression, but ignored it. She couldn't believe she was going to have a hand in the next book by bestseller

J. L. Allan. "I didn't know you were Spanish. I mean that J. L. Allan was Spanish."

"My mother is American. That market is larger than Spain, though the books have been translated into Spanish." He turned back to his desk. "I don't usually write here, so the place will be yours during the day. Maria started at ten and worked until six. Will those hours suit you?"

"I'm a morning person, could I start earlier?"

"Whatever works. There's a lot to catch up on. The completed manuscript is due in another month. I've finished the first draft, but need the transcriptions before I can edit the work. I'll take what you finish each day, make notations and return it to you. If I could have them done by the next day, it would help."

"Sure." She hoped she could figure out the computer, the printer and read his handwriting, but she let none of her doubts show. She was almost giddy with excitement. Wait until her friends heard who she was working for!

The reality returned. Not that she could tell anyone—at least not now. News like that would spread like wildfire and her dad was sure to hear. It wouldn't take him two seconds to have someone track down J. L. Allan and find her.

Would working for J. L. Allan give her some pointers in unraveling the mystery in her own life? She wondered if she dare share her quest with him. Would he be scornful, or helpful? It was too early to tell. Time enough to ask for help once she decided if she really wanted to proceed in locating her mother or not. There were dangers in revealing the past. Would she like what she found?

As Rachel approached the kitchen early the next morning, she heard the murmur of voices. The housekeeper was obviously back. Esperenza, was that the name Luis had said?

She slowed, not wanting to interrupt without knowing if the conversation was private. She could hear Luis quite clearly as he told Esperenza to keep quiet about everything.

The woman sounded comfortable in arguing with the man.

"What is there to hide? It is all in the newspapers."

"Just don't tell her anything. And if she questions you, let me know immediately."

"Curiosity is natural in women," she replied.

"About the job, maybe. But not me."

"Oh, Luis. It is time to put the sadness behind and move on. Go to America and celebrate the new book. Visit friends and family. Forget the past and find a new woman."

"Esperenza, your kindness does you credit. I'm satisfied with my life the way it is. I do not wish it disrupted. Understand? No answering questions."

"*Si,* I understand."

Rachel heard his step a moment before the door swung open. She had enough time to take a step back and then look as if she'd been walking forward all along. She paused and smiled innocently at Luis. "Good morning."

He looked at her for a moment then nodded curtly, striding past her.

Rachel continued into the kitchen, feeling as if she'd fallen down the rabbit hole. What kind of secret might the housekeeper tell a perfect stranger?

"Buenos Dias, señorita," the older woman called to Rachel upon spotting her. "I am Esperenza. Señor Alvares said you are Señorita Rachel Goodson. Welcome. Are you ready for breakfast?"

"Yes, thank you. I'm happy to meet you."

"Ah, Americano, like la Señora. You will want a big breakfast, not just bread and coffee. Where will you eat? On the patio? Or the dining room?"

"Here is fine," Rachel said. The thought of sitting alone in the vast dining room she'd seen from the doorway in the hall was not appealing. It looked large enough to hold state dinners.

"Has Señor Alvares already eaten?" she asked.

"*Si.* He rises before dawn most days. He works in Benidorm and always wishes to arrive early. Come, sit. I will prepare breakfast. Do you start with coffee?"

"That would be great." Rachel's curiosity was running rampant. So her new boss had something to hide. Mysteries abounded everywhere. What was his? And if he went to the Consortium's offices in Benidorm, why hadn't he taken his writing in for the secretaries there to transcribe?

Writers were eccentric. It was the only answer.

She'd been up late. It had been several years since she'd read *Night into Day*. She'd enjoyed it almost as much last night as when she'd first read it, even though she'd remembered partway through who the killer was. It was fun to know the ending and see the clever way Luis had led the reader on. The clues were subtle. Only by searching for them could she find how he wove the plot so skillfully to fool the reader until the very end.

"Where are you from in America?" Esperenza asked as she began preparing an omelet. Rachel remembered her own meal the night before. Never could get too many omelets, she thought.

"California."

"Ah, I know it. I have been to Hollywood."

"You have? Did you star in a movie?" Rachel asked, smiling.

"No, no, I went with Señora Bonita before her death." She crossed herself, her expression turning sad for a moment. "California is—extravagant."

"Yes, it is. That and more. Who was Señora Bonita? Was she Luis's mother?" Rachel frowned. That couldn't be right. Luis talked as if his mother were still alive when he mentioned her. Another thought took hold. Would Esperenza dash to Luis to tell him Rachel had asked a question?

"Ah no. La Señora is still living. She and her second husband are in Cannes. She loves the beach. After the tragedy, she remarried and moved away. She is from Iowa. Do you know that state?"

"I know of it, of course. But I've never been there," Rachel said, growing confused. What tragedy?

"Luis, he went to school in the United States. But not Iowa. His mother lived in California when she left here. Is there something wrong with Iowa?"

Rachel shook her head. ''No, but it is not extravagant like California. Very quiet life-style. Maybe she wanted more for her son.''

Esperenza looked pensive. ''Maybe he should have gone there to study, to stay with his grandparents. Maybe everything would have turned out differently. Ah, who is to know.'' She placed an artfully arranged plate before Rachel. In addition to the fresh fruit and fluffy omelet, there was lightly buttered toast. Rachel looked at the plate. There was enough food to feed a family of three.

''Such a tragedy,'' Rachel murmured, giving her attention to her meal, but hoping the lack of questions would open flood gates. At least Esperenza couldn't complain to her employer that Rachel had questioned her.

''Ah, it was. After Señora Bonita's death, I thought he would go mad with grief. He raged, and refused to have anything to do with old friends. He has shut himself away from all the old routines. Three years have passed, but still the silence encases this house. Still he mourns. It is not right. He needs to move on to life and happiness. Find another wife. Have children.''

Luis? Somehow Rachel couldn't envision her new employer full of happiness. The brooding intensity suited his dark looks. She tried to picture the man in love, and failed. Still, how awful to lose his wife. She couldn't have been very old. What had the woman been like? Something very special if Luis mourned her death three years later.

"He swears he will never again marry. But how will he ever have children? Who will fill this house with laughter if not young children?" She shook her head and refilled Rachel's cup with fragrant coffee.

Careful, Rachel admonished herself. She wanted more information, but refused to ask the questions that bubbled. Hadn't she heard Esperenza mention newspaper accounts? Maybe she could learn more from that source, if she could find a library in this small village.

At least speculating about Luis took her mind off her father for a while, Rachel thought as she headed for the study after eating as much of the breakfast as she could manage.

Entering, she went to her desk, surprised to recognize the software program Maria used for word processing. It was the same one Rachel used at home. In California, she corrected herself. She no longer considered her father's house her home.

Luis's handwriting wasn't the best in the world, but she could read it easily enough. Soon she was engrossed in the story and typed as fast as she was able to keep up with the reading. She was coming in after the beginning and wished she could read the opening pages to get the background she was missing. Even so, the story was captivating.

"I'm going, now," Luis said from the doorway.

Rachel broke her concentration and looked at him. She thought he'd already left. "To Benidorm, right?"

He nodded. Slipping a piece of paper on her desk, he said, "That's the number of the office. Call if you run into problems. I need you to concentrate on the manuscript."

"Got it." She could make some inroads if that was all she had to do today, though her typing wasn't that fast. Still, whatever she could do was more than had been done yesterday.

Time was suspended as she was drawn further into the twists and turns of the plot. The man was brilliant. No wonder his books were so enjoyed. She couldn't wait to see what happened next.

''It is bad enough to have to chase after Luis when he is home during the day, but I expected you to be at lunch on time,'' Esperenza said from the doorway.

Rachel looked up, blinked. She glanced at her watch. It was after one! Where had the morning gone? She looked at the small stack of turned over pages. That's where. She'd taken a short break around ten, but beyond that, she'd been at the computer nonstop. She wasn't a very fast typist, but did her best to be accurate. More uniformity and clarity in Luis's handwriting might have helped.

Stretching, she tried to loosen her neck and shoulder muscles. She felt so stiff. No wonder. Hours without a break would do that.

''Sorry, Esperenza. I didn't realize it was so late.''

''Tsk, tsk, do not get like Luis. I don't have the energy these days to chase after you both!'' the older woman grumbled as she walked back down the hall.

''I have served lunch on the terrace. Take a walk, maybe siesta, then work.'' Grumbling even more about people not eating, she disappeared into the kitchen.

''What terrace?'' Rachel asked, looking over her shoulder at the patio outside the French doors. There was nothing but the flagstone.

Good grief, she'd either have to get Esperenza to take her there, or find it on her own. The *castillo* was bigger than she'd first thought. Not only were there the twenty-seven bedrooms Luis had mentioned, but at least two formal sitting rooms, the huge state dining room that would easily seat fifty guests, and numerous other rooms and corridors she hadn't explored.

All for one man?

A huge family wouldn't fill up the place, but at least every kid could have friends over without infringing on anyone's space.

She peered into the dining room. Through the opened doors she spotted the fluttering of a tablecloth on the terrazzo terrace beyond. Hurrying through the room, she stepped into the shaded area. A round table had been set for one. Rachel sat down and began to eat. The chicken salad was delicious, as were the warm rolls. Esperenza had even made iced tea.

Rachel was glad for the break, and in such a lovely setting. Did Luis ever entertain? Fill the lower floor with laughter, discussions and music? Not recently, according to his housekeeper. But she whiled away the time thinking of elegant Spanish couples being entertained on a grand scale.

All too soon, she'd finished and returned to the study. She could have taken a longer break, but Rachel wanted to see what came next in the book. She was not even a tenth of the way through the stack of yellow papers. It would be days before she was caught up. But she was being entertained every moment.

At the end of the day, Rachel's shoulders ached and she had a slight headache. Hoping to clear her head, she went for another walk around the grounds, pausing to study the rows of olive trees that stretched to the horizon. It was quiet. Did the atmosphere change when olives were being harvested? Was it done by hand, or did huge machines crawl over the land, plucking olives from the limbs? She had a better picture of joyful workers swarming over the trees as they did in California, laughing and shouting as they worked the fields. When were olives harvested? She'd probably be long gone by then.

After freshening up for dinner, Rachel was directed by Esperenza back to the terrace where she'd had lunch.

Luis was seated, reading a newspaper. He rose when he saw her and inclined his head gravely, indicating the second chair.

Slipping into it, Rachel rushed into speech. "I'm sorry if I kept you waiting. Esperenza said dinner was at seven and it's just seven now." She wasn't sure she liked the idea of sharing a meal with her boss. Whatever would they talk about?

"I have not been waiting." He folded the paper and put it on an adjacent chair.

"The story is fantastic. I was so caught up in it, the entire day flew by. Where can I find the opening pages? I want to read it all," Rachel said. She had not been able to figure out which file Maria had saved the opening chapters to. She would search every one if necessary, but if he discovered her searching through the computer, he'd believe her to be searching for incriminating evidence of something. If he just told her which file, it would save time and effort and misunderstanding.

"So it starts," he murmured.

"So what starts?" Rachel asked, placing her napkin in her lap and looking at the array of food on the table. Rice was piled high. Fresh fruit salad in a strawberry sauce tantalized. The roast looked cooked to perfection.

"I don't care for flattery. I'm not in the market for a romance. I have everything I want in my life as it is right now. Do the work and when Maria returns, leave," he said.

Rachel looked him, stunned by his rudeness and assumptions.

"Now wait a minute! I'm not flattering you. The book is darn good. You must know it from how well the others were received. And if you think I have the slightest interest in romance, guess again. Why you think any woman would want to deal with you is beyond me. That brooding Heathcliff demeanor might appeal to some, but not me. I want laughter and fun, not gloom and doom. Maybe I had better eat in the kitchen with the rest of the help." She threw her napkin on the table and made to rise.

His hand gripped her wrist. "No. Please sit."

For a moment Rachel resisted. His clasp wasn't unbreakable, just firm. Would he release her if she yanked away?

"I refuse to sit here and be insulted," she said haughtily.

"I...apologize." He released her arm. "I believe I jumped to an erroneous conclusion."

"Well, for a hotshot writer of detection, your own powers don't seem so great. I'm not out to flirt with you, or do some kind of expose. I'm not some groupie flattering you for some attention. I only want a job. A temporary job.''

''For which you have no papers.''

She swallowed and tried to keep her gaze locked firmly with his as if it wasn't the major problem it could become.

''Papers?'' As a dissembler, Rachel feared she was inept.

His look turned speculative. ''The story has a lot of work ahead before it's ready for the publisher. Even when the first draft is transcribed, there'll be revisions, editing. Check the list of files Maria has on the computer, there should be one called City. That's the working title of the book, *City Nights*. Would you care for rice?''

Rachel was startled at the abrupt change of topic. She expected to be on her way out by now. Insulting her was one thing. Ignoring her lack of work papers was another. Did he need secretarial help that badly? She didn't think so. He'd managed without for several weeks, he could have done so for longer. Or made use of someone in his business office.

She took the bowl, her fingers trembling slightly. Desperately hoping he wouldn't notice, she served herself and then began to eat. The food almost caught in her throat, but she hoped her demeanor appeared as calm and controlled as his.

Gradually the awkwardness evaporated. She looked around, searching for something to spark a normal, calm conversation. They were at the side of the house and from this angle could not see the Mediterranean Sea. Instead, banks of flowers bordered the patio with colorful red and pink blossoms. There were a few small white buds on one bush. The air felt warm, even though they sat beneath a trellis which would have shaded them completely from the late afternoon sun had the *castillo* not already done so.

It was a lovely setting. One she would have enjoyed a lot more without the brooding presence of her boss. Maybe tomorrow she'd see about eating her meals on her own or with Esperenza.

That reminded her of breakfast and the limited revelations she'd been given. Would

Esperenza open up after knowing Rachel better? She wasn't a reporter. She wasn't planning to sell some story and make a fabulous amount of money. But she was curious as to why Luis thought she could do so. Unless he'd murdered his wife. Which was highly unlikely. Otherwise, what dark secrets did he hold?

"Tell me about yourself," Luis said a few moments later. "Are you vacationing in Spain?"

"Yes." Sort of.

He waited patiently, his eyes never leaving hers.

"I've always wanted to visit Spain. I studied Spanish for years in California. So I thought I would be ready when I arrived, but it's a bit daunting. I've been to Segovia, and to Toledo. And of course, Granada and the Alhambra. I could have lived there, I think."

"It is lovely to look at, but think of the inconveniences—no indoor plumbing, no microwaves."

She looked at him. Was he actually conversing with her? Amazing.

"Of course I never think about that. I imagine only the glorious times. With my luck, I'd have been the scullery maid or something, not the pampered daughter of the palace. But it's so lovely and impressive. Imagine what it must have been like in its prime."

"A romantic," he scoffed gently.

"Better than being a cynic," she returned, thinking of her father and Paul.

"You find me cynical?" he asked.

Rachel shrugged. "I don't know you, señor. We have hardly had time to exchange philosophies. But I'd bet you are. Aren't most men?"

"Only those who have seen the world as it is," he replied easily.

"Where did you go to school?" she asked.

He raised an eyebrow at the question.

"Esperenza mentioned at breakfast that your mother is from Iowa, and that you went to school in the States. That's why your English is so good, isn't it? Otherwise how could you write novels in the language?"

"What else did Esperenza mention at breakfast?" he asked silkily.

"Not much," she was suddenly aware of the trap. Why couldn't she learn to think before she spoke?

"If you wish to know something about me, ask me, not my housekeeper." His voice was cold as stone.

"I didn't ask her anything, she volunteered the information." She didn't want to get the other woman in trouble.

"You expect me to believe she didn't mention our great tragedy? How my wife was killed in a horrible car accident? How I grieve and mourn her passing?" The mocking tone in his voice was pronounced. Rachel suspected it wasn't the first time Esperenza had expounded on the event.

He rose and leaned so close Rachel drew back a few inches. The anger pouring from his eyes was enough to drown her.

"If you value working where papers are not required, stay out of my life," he said very slowly, very clearly.

"Or?" she challenged recklessly.

"There are many ways to end things, remember that." His gaze held hers without wavering.

Rachel watched, shivering in the warm spring air. She felt helpless to look away. The strength of his will was formidable. He had obviously loved his wife a great deal to protect her memory at all costs.

For an instant, Rachel envied a dead woman. What would it be like to be loved so much? To be the happy recipient of all that intensity. To know a man would do anything to keep her happy.

She cleared her throat. "I apologize, Señor, if I stepped out of line. I didn't question Esperenza about your personal life and in future will refrain from listening if she begins to talk."

The tension that was thick enough to cut with a knife gradually eased. He nodded abruptly once and resumed his seat as if nothing had happened.

Rachel wondered how long it would be until she could leave without it appearing as if she were running away. Too long. Every second seemed like an eternity.

She tried to eat, but the food clogged in her throat. She took a sip of iced tea. It helped ease the tightness but not enough. Toying with her food, she hoped Luis would not notice. She had enough with her own family matters to deal with. She was not trying to pry into his. Could she continue to work with him? Not unless they came to an understanding. If he continued to think she was a spy, she couldn't remain no matter how much she needed the money. But how to convince him she wasn't a threat to him or the memory of his wife?

CHAPTER THREE

THE MEAL BLESSEDLY came to an end a short time later when Esperenza came to tell Luis he had a phone call. Without a word to Rachel, he rose and went inside. She exhaled as if she'd been holding her breath.

"The food is not to your liking?" Esperenza asked, noting the amount remaining on Rachel's plate.

"It's delicious. We, er, were talking and I just haven't had a chance to eat," Rachel said, loathed to have Esperenza guess the topic of conversation.

The housekeeper nodded and returned inside, leaving Rachel alone with her own thoughts.

"Great, I've managed to tick off possibly the only employer between here and Madrid who wouldn't ask for a working visa. Must be a knack," she murmured, taking another bite of the delicious roast. With her disturbing boss gone, she was able to enjoy the meal.

His chastisement didn't erase her curiosity, however. She wondered what his wife had been like. What their life together had been like. Obviously a great love story. Unlike the planned marriage her father had insisted upon. If she had given in, would she ever have grown to love Paul? Or would theirs have been a marriage that grew cold and distant over time?

And what of her father's own marriage? What had caused that ending? How could he have lied to her all her life?

The disquieting thought of her mother ignoring her for more than twenty years would not be quelled. She knew where Rachel lived, why hadn't she tried to get in touch with her only daughter? Maybe not immediately after she left, but later, when Rachel had been a teenager?

Or *was* she her mother's only child? Had she married again, raised a family with someone else?

Rachel wished she knew more—more of her own family, and more about her mysterious employer. Her father had refused to say anything about her mother except Rachel was better off not knowing her. She had so many questions, and he hadn't answered a single one. Instead he'd been furious she'd even brought up the subject once she'd discovered their divorce papers, railing at her for meddling into things that were not her concern.

As if longing for her mother had nothing to do with her. She could understand bitterness between partners after a divorce, but to deny her very existence to her own daughter was not something Rachel could fathom, much less condone.

Luis's edict not withstanding, she planned to see what she could find from local papers at her first chance. Maybe she'd get some answers at least to one mystery.

Rachel headed for the study the next morning with some trepidation. She felt awkward after their confrontation at dinner. Luis was on the phone when she slipped into her chair and pulled up the transcription she'd been doing yesterday. The stack of yellow paper had barely diminished. There was still a huge stack of pages to go before she caught up. More than she could do in several weeks at the rate she was going. Maybe practice would accelerate her typing, though she strove for accuracy more than speed at this point.

Much as she tried to focus on the work at hand, she was distracted by her employer. She could see him from the corner of her eye. He leaned back in his chair, his speech rapid and colloquial. She had some difficulty understanding it, not that she was eavesdropping, but it was hard to ignore his strong voice when they were separated by only a few feet of space.

He seemed to be arguing with someone about appearing at an event, she gathered. Trying to concentrate on the transcription, she wasn't drawn into the story like she had been yesterday. The sound of his voice took precedence.

Finally he hung up. With a short expletive, he rose and paced the room. Warily Rachel watched him.

He turned and looked right at her.

"I've been pressured to speak at fiesta next week," he said angrily, as if it were her fault. "A friend of mine is mayor of the town. He insists."

Luis spun around and stalked across the room to the opened French doors, gazing out. "I have refused the last three times he's asked. This time he says he won't take no for an answer."

Rachel was surprised anyone could stand up to Luis if he said no. She waited. Was he just thinking aloud, or did he need some secretarial assistance? He was a writer, so probably didn't need help with a speech. She wished she had a true background in office work, maybe then she'd know where he was leading, why he was telling her all this.

He turned and walked to her desk.

"I want you to accompany me to the fiesta."

That was the last thing she expected. "If you need me to, of course." Was she to take notes? Carry his appointment book?

He nodded, letting his gaze drift over her hair, his perusal going down to where the desk cut off his view. ''I do not wish to be the target of every matchmaker and groupie in attendance. If I arrive with a date, they will leave me alone. At least, I hope so.'' He shrugged. ''Time will tell. It will be next Thursday night. We'll leave here shortly before seven. I do not plan to stay late.''

''Fine.'' Did all secretarial jobs include this kind of work? How many groupies could the village hold? It wasn't a large place to begin with. As to matchmakers, she wasn't sure her presence would stop anyone.

''Uh, how dressy is this?'' She had packed light when she'd left home. She had no dress fancy enough for a party. She'd have to use some of her precious Euros to buy something suitable for the event if needed.

''Not dressy. It's fiesta, a parade, eating from food stands in the streets, crowds, loud music, fireworks.''

''Why do you need to go?'' she asked. ''It doesn't sound as if it's your favorite activity.''

''The olive groves are mine. There are a lot of workers who live in the village. The mayor wants an appearance for a pep talk, essentially a lord of the manor type thing. 'Thank you for your hard work. This year will be the best ever.' I'm sure you know the drill.''

She suspected his wife's death had kept him from going in years past. Each person grieved in his or her own way and time. But after three years, maybe he should venture forth a bit. Life did, after all, move on.

Even when someone hadn't died, she thought wryly. The pang hit again, the anguish and disbelief. She still hadn't thought of how to proceed. Maybe instead of unraveling the mystery of her boss and his past, she should concentrate on her own.

Luis snapped the briefcase shut and lifted it. ''If Juan or Julian call, tell them I'm on my way into the office.''

After a solitary dinner that evening, Rachel was at loose ends. She had her wish to dine alone, but not because of anything she'd said. Luis had not returned when Esperenza served the meal. He'd been delayed, the housekeeper explained.

Rachel's neck and shoulders ached from the long day at the computer. She was quite a few more pages along, and enjoying the story more and more. She'd found the file Maria had started and printed out the first several chapters to read later tonight. Tomorrow she'd be up to speed on the story line. It would help in transcribing the rest. And in satisfying her curiosity.

Once again, Rachel sought relaxation after dinner by wandering around the grounds, enjoying the early evening. The setting sun painted the sky a brilliant rose and pink. The gentle breeze carried sweet fragrances from the blossoms surrounding her. The grounds were private—the perfect place for someone in hiding. She frowned. She preferred to think of it as retrenching.

Soon she'd go into the village, or to Benidorm to contact her friend Caroline. She had checked the computer she was using, but there was no e-mail connection. While she was angry at her father, she didn't wish him to worry needlessly. She'd contacted her best friend via e-mail when she'd first arrived in

Spain to ask her to call her father to let him know she was safe.

She knew it placed Caroline in an awkward position, but it gave her a crucial buffer. When she thought about it, she and Luis had something in common—both requiring a buffer against the situations they were in.

Exploring the grounds more fully tonight, she rounded a hedge and found an old stone wall. The flat stones had been matched and placed so close together no mortar had been needed. It looked old, but substantial. Who had built it? In the distance she could see where flowers grew near the base.

Sitting on the top, she lifted her legs over until they dangled on the far side where the ground slopped away. The stones were still warm from the sun. She could easily see the sea from this position and the spread of olive trees extending to the horizon. Gradually dusk fell.

The lights in the village came on. She imagined families eating together, laughing, sharing the day's events. Wistfully she wished for such an end to the day. But even when she'd been a child, her father rarely ate dinner at home. Business was all-consuming for him. Late nights working, or entertaining clients. When she grew old enough, she began to attend such functions with him. But in thinking back, she couldn't remember a time when just she and her dad had gone somewhere for fun. Never once had they done anything not connected to growing the business. It paid off; he was a wealthy man. But what had he lost along the way?

"I wondered where you were," Luis said coming out of the darkness.

"It's so peaceful and serene here," she said, gazing at the village below. The lights sparkled, some reflecting off the pier onto the water.

"It's even more beautiful during fiesta. Lights are strung around doors and windows, across the streets and outlining businesses. The fireworks are brilliant."

"Do you watch them from here?" she asked.

"I used to." He fell silent. Gazing off into the past, she suspected.

''But we will see them from the village next week, won't we?'' she said practically.

''Unless we can get away before they start.'' He rested a hip against the stone wall. Rachel glanced at him, not seeing much as the night grew darker. He wore black again. Was it because he was in mourning, or did he like the color?

''Tell me about Rachel Goodson,'' he said.

She grew instantly alert. Why was he asking? She thought he'd been satisfied with her answers before.

''There's not much to tell. I grew up in California. Came to Spain.''

''And now you're working without permits, right?''

''I don't have any, it's true. But I don't know of any reason I couldn't get the permits given enough time. I didn't apply.''

''Planning on vacationing only?''

''And fell in love with Spain, so I want to stay as long as possible.''

He was silent a moment then spoke softly, ''Why do I feel there is more?''

Because there is, and you are very astute, she wanted to say, but dared not. Men stuck together. He'd probably insist she call her father, or phone him directly himself. Despite his own love match, would he see merit in her father's idea of a dynastic marriage? In the old days, Spanish nobility had married for wealth, land and position. It was entrenched in their history.

"Perhaps you see mysteries where none exist," she said. "How do you come up with your stories?"

"I do not murder people to get authenticity," he said wryly.

She laughed. "I never thought you did. Why would I?"

"Someone suggested it once."

"You're kidding."

"An American, actually, at a book signing tour my publisher talked me into. I guess he couldn't figure out how else I could come up with such realism."

"I don't see you being talked into anything," she mused.

She felt his gaze.

"It happens. Like fiesta."

"That sounds like a favor for a friend."

"I wanted to stay on the good side of my publisher, back then, too."

"So it must have been an early book. I would expect any publisher in the free world would love to have you as an author these days, on whatever terms you dictate. Your books sell terrifically well."

He said nothing.

"Oops, was that groupie mentality?" Rachel wanted to laugh. Couldn't he take some things as they were meant, without looking for hidden meanings behind everything?

"Did you mean it as flattery?"

"No, I meant it as fact. I understand a lot about the bottom line and what contributes to it."

"Business background?"

"Sort of. I learned a lot from my father," she said reluctantly.

"What does your father do?"

Warning bells sounded. "He's in business."

"What business?"

Someone born and raised in Spain would likely not have heard of the conglomerate her father headed. But someone who had spent his educational years in the States probably would have. Would knowing that raise even more questions?

"A word of advice," he said, amusement sounding in his tone. "If you don't wish to make a mystery of things, have a ready answer to questions. Even if it's wrong, it'll put people off the scent. My curiosity is piqued by your reluctance to talk about your father. Are you two estranged?"

"You could say that."

"Does he know you are here?"

"Here in your home, or here in Spain?"

"Either?"

She hesitated another moment. "It's really not any concern of yours, señor, is it?" She swung her legs over the wall and jumped down. He rose and stood beside her, a dark shadow in the darker night.

"When a young woman is living in my household, all her concerns are mine."

''I'm your secretary—your temporary secretary. That doesn't give you any special responsibility toward me or what I'm doing. And if staying here makes a difference, I'll find a room in the village. Good night.'' She started for the house hoping he wouldn't follow. So what if his interest was piqued. Let him stew in his own curiosity. She had a quest to pursue and it was not his business nor that of her father how she accomplished her ends.

Being in Spain was delaying the implementation of her plans. She should have begun the search for her mother immediately upon learning she had not died. But she wasn't sure she wanted to find her. Once Maria returned, Rachel would go back to the U.S. and begin her search in earnest. If she located her mother, she didn't have to meet her. Was there a way to find out more about the entire situation before blundering into the midst of it? Who could she trust to tell her the truth?

Luis watched as Rachel walked to the house without looking back. When she rounded the hedge and was lost from view, he sat again on the wall and glanced toward the village. She was right, she was not his concern. But for the first time in many years, he felt interest in another person.

Her blond hair was sunshine in the night. Her blue eyes fascinated him. She was a mixture of enticing femininity and baffling standoffishness. American bravado and appealing fascination with Spain.

It was as if he'd been in a cave for three years, unwilling to walk into the light of day. But Rachel cracked the walls. He wasn't sure why, but he wanted to talk with her. Learn more about her. Listen to her fractured Spanish. He recognized the Mexican influence in her speech and found it charming. Maybe he should speak English to make her feel more at home, but she never asked, and he liked her accent.

He liked her honest way of looking at him. Not sexy and flirtatious like Bonita. Not flattering and oozing with false sincerity like the groupies he'd met at parties and book tours when he and Bonita went to the States the first few years of his writing success.

Since her death, he'd done all he could to avoid everyone, man and woman alike. Maybe as Esperenza was fond of saying, it was time to move on.

Not that he planned anything more than a work relationship with his unexpected secretary. But trying to piece together the various components of her life was proving interesting. Rachel Goodson was hiding something. And he suddenly realized he wanted to discover what it was.

He knew she was not a reporter—at least not like any he'd ever met. And she didn't play the part of groupie. She said flattering things, but he was beginning to suspect she meant them. Which meant she was a genuine fan. He should watch himself around her, no use alienating a reader.

He almost smiled, as if he'd cared who he'd alienated lately.

He looked over where he knew the olive grove began. The land had been in his family for generations. His father had wanted more children, but he and his mother had only had the two of them, he and his sister Sophia. And he'd lost his father far too young. Not before the man had instilled the love and responsibility of the family estates in his only son, however. Still, the man should have lived another thirty years or more. Would he have advice to give today?

When had the responsibility become such a burden? Was it Bonita's death and all that involved? Before? Or only since, when he wished he could leave Spain never to return?

Rising, he wondered where in California his mysterious guest lived. And speculated with a dozen scenarios as to why she was reticent about her father.

Her eyes flashed fire sometimes. He found himself planning some outrageous thing to say next to spark that fire. Would the flash be there if he kissed her?

The thought struck him like a hammer. Maybe Esperenza's wish was about to come true. Maybe, to a limited degree, he could move forward.

As far as taking the delectable Miss Goodson to bed?

He was out of practice at flirting with a beautiful woman. But like riding a bike, it was not something totally forgotten. Would she agree to an affair? It would be safe, no lasting tangles, no devotion, no love. He wouldn't open himself up to that again. Rachel would be gone as soon as Maria returned. A clean break.

His idea to use her as a buffer from those who might try to get close at fiesta was a start. He'd do his best to make the evening enjoyable and see where things went.

No danger in her heart becoming involved. She was on vacation. A romantic fling with a Spaniard would probably give her endless stories to tell her friends when she returned to California.

He considered the various aspects as he headed back to the castle. In the morning, he'd implement stage one to see if he could find out if Rachel would be at all receptive to the idea.

At breakfast the next morning, Rachel was careful to keep the conversation with Esperenza neutral. She was not going to get into hot water with her employer today! Sipping the thick hot chocolate, she nibbled on the fresh baked bread. It was Friday. Would she have a chance to get to the village tomorrow?

"Is there a library in town?" she asked the housekeeper.

"No. There is a fine bookstore near the café. It carries some books for tourists, and newspapers. They are all in Spanish, but there is an English store in Benidorm."

No library? That could be a setback. "How about an Internet café somewhere nearby?"

"*Si,* in Benidorm. There is a big library there, too. It is required to be a resident to borrow books, however."

Books weren't what she was interested in. Would the library have past issues of the local paper? Or would she have to visit the newspaper office directly to research the incident she had in mind?

Three years ago. Sort of vague. Was it exactly three years ago so she could start with the same month, or would she have to review all twelve months? She wished she had just a scrap more to go on.

"Is there a bus to Benidorm?" she asked. "I expect to have tomorrow free. I thought I'd go sightseeing."

"There is a bus. It leaves early. You don't need to ride the bus. Ask Señor Luis for a car. There are three in the garage."

"Three cars?"

"One is his, the other's his mother's. I use the third."

Did she dare ask to borrow a car? Would he think her out of her mind?

"Maria has her own car, I take it."

"*Si.* It is in the village until she returns. La Señora won't be visiting any time soon. Her car just sits idle between her visits."

"Maybe I will ask then," she said. When pigs fly. Or when I get enough courage to beard the lion.

Entering the office a short time later, Rachel greeted Luis, surprised to see him sitting behind his desk. Books were scattered across the wooden surface, many lying open.

Taking her seat, Rachel looked at the stack of yellow pages. Surely it had diminished from yesterday morning, hadn't it?

Glancing at her boss, she saw he was engrossed in his reading. Wasn't he going into Benidorm today? "Research?" she guessed.

"Various poisons," he murmured absently.

Rachel sat behind the terminal and began transcribing his words onto the computer. She was more and more fascinated with the man as she typed the words he'd written. What a complex mixture of astute businessman and hardcore mystery writer.

The morning passed swiftly and to her surprise—pleasantly. She glanced up once in a while to study Luis. His concentration seemed total. He jotted notes, exchanged books, and read without seeming to notice his surroundings.

The third time she looked up, his gaze met hers.

"Do you have a question?" he asked.

"No, just taking a break." She rose and stretched, rolling her head round, trying to ease the kinks. "You don't have to go to Benidorm today?"

"No."

"So you don't go every day?"

"No." He closed the book he was reading, tossed the pen down. "Perhaps a short walk to clear your mind," he suggested.

"That sounds nice." She headed for the French doors. He rose as she neared.

"I'll join you. Researching obscure poisons and then trying to figure out how it would be obtained by the villain is hard work."

"Not as hard as the writing, I'd think," she said. "Where do you write?"

"I have a car and driver to get to and from work. When business needs aren't pressing, I write as Marcos drives. Sometimes I take a day off to work here. There's a place nearby where I compose my books when the weather is suitable. The rewrites and polishing I do at the desk, and usually hand off the pages to Maria as soon as I've marked them up. But to think, to conceptualize and write down the ideas, I don't want interruptions."

"How close is the place nearby?"

He hesitated a moment, then nodded toward a path that meandered away from the terrace. "Come, I'll show you."

Rachel walked beside him as they started up the incline behind the castle. The path narrowed as they steadily climbed. She glanced at the man beside her, wondering if he'd been cloned. This was not the terse, suspicious man of the last couple of days. He was almost friendly.

When they reached the summit, Rachel stopped and looked around in pleasure. The view was terrific. Behind her was the sea, ahead of her more olive groves, and in the far distance, mountains rising. From left to right, she could see the entire horizon.

"Spectacular," she said reverently.

"The gazebo is where I write," he said pointing to a small structure a few yards away. He led the way and when she stepped inside, she was delighted. There were a couple of chairs, tables with pencils and pads of paper and a large chaise lounge. The view was magnificent. She was amazed he could compose the convoluted stories he wrote from here. Any time he paused, he had only to look up and gaze into forever.

How did he come up with such dark stories of murder and intrigue? She'd only want to write epics to encompass the vast expanse before her.

"How do you get any work done? I'd stare at the view all day," she said, moving around the gazebo, checking out the scene from each archway.

"It is new to you. Sad to say, if you lived here much of your life you would take it for granted. It has always been there. It will always be there. I can ignore it."

"I guess," she said, gazing at the beauty surrounding her. It would take her a long time to take such a vista for granted.

"Come whenever you wish. Just follow the path."

She turned. "Really?" It sounded very generous—not something she'd expect him to offer. "Thank you. I may do that."

"Mi casa es tu casa," he said softly.

She took a breath and boldly asked, "May I also borrow a car to drive to Benidorm tomorrow? I assume I get weekends off and I thought I'd like to see some more of Spain.''

His hesitation was slight. Rachel wasn't sure if she'd imagined it. ''It would be fine to borrow the car when you wish. I will show you where we keep the keys. However, as it happens, I'm going to Benidorm myself in the morning. To check up on things I missed staying home today. I can drive you there, show you the way, so next time you will know it.''

''I couldn't impose,'' she said, suddenly wary about being in his company longer than she needed to be. There was something about the man that was creeping beneath her defenses. She needed to keep a professional distance.

''No imposition. I planned to leave at eight. Is that too early?''

''No, that's fine. And if you can show me the bus terminal, I can find my way back.''

''Nonsense. I will bring you back.''

''But—''

''I insist.'' The steely tone squelched any resistance. Even when being kind, he came across as autocratic. She thought about arguing the point, but it wasn't worth it. She would appreciate the ride, why not admit it?

Would he want to know what she planned to do in the city, or simply drop her at some plaza and arrange to pick her up at some mutually convenient time? How did someone explain her father had lied to her all her life and now she was going to take the first steps to find her mother?

"Thank you. I appreciate that." She smiled politely, her smile fading at the intensity of his gaze. His dark eyes seemed to see straight into her. Her heart rate increased slightly and she felt a warmth invade her. They were in the shade of the gazebo's roof. It wasn't sunshine warming her blood.

"I better get back," she said. Was that breathless tone hers? He'd offered her a ride, not a marriage proposal. What was the matter with her?

"Esperenza will have lunch ready before long," he said, stepping aside to let her lead the way.

Descending the path was even easier than the gentle climb had been. Before long they were at the terrace and entering the study.

"Thank you for showing me the gazebo," she said.

He stopped beside her, reaching out to brush a strand of blond hair from her cheek. Her heart skipped a beat at the unexpected touch. Was it her imagination, or had his fingers lingered? It seemed a very personal gesture. If she didn't watch it, she'd become the groupie he sometimes thought her.

"I'll wash up before lunch," she said, to escape before her foolish thoughts morphed into something more.

Promptly at eight the next morning Rachel descended the stairs. Luis was waiting in the foyer.

"Good morning," she said feeling a flutter of anticipation at his dark looks when his eyes looked at her.

"Did you sleep well?"

"Like a baby." Once she fell asleep. Of course that wasn't easy with all the thoughts of yesterday cramming for first place in her mind last night.

"And you?"

"As always. I don't require a great deal of sleep," he said opening the front door. "The car is ready. Esperenza said you had not eaten. Do you wish something before we go?"

"No, I'll find something there."

"Do you have any place special you'd like me to drop you?"

"Center of town would be great. I'll look for a café to have a *café con leche* and some rolls." Hopefully a café with Internet connection. She could eat if she had to wait, or log on immediately if there was a terminal available.

Stepping outside, she spotted the black convertible. She smiled. The weather was perfect. Her hair would get blown, but it didn't matter. She would relish the feel of the warm wind against her face, and the freedom of riding in an open car.

He drove down the winding mountain road with ease. Rachel couldn't help contrasting the wild ride up in the taxicab with the control with which Luis handled the car. She didn't feel a bit afraid with him at the wheel. Instead she settled back to enjoy herself.

She did her best to ignore her companion. Which wasn't easy with him only inches away. He seemed to fill most of the space in the car and she was acutely aware of his presence. The musky scent of his aftershave blew by in the wind. The smooth movement of his hands as he shifted the gears drew her attention. His strong jaw, dark hair, the black clothes, completed him. She couldn't see his eyes because of the dark glasses he wore, but she knew what they would be like, slightly mocking, turning to angry intensity if something displeased him.

"I can still get a ride back on the bus if your business will take all day," she said as they swept through the village and took the highway toward Benidorm.

"I said I'd drive you back. How long do you plan to be?" he said with a hint of edge to his tone.

"I don't know. I thought I'd just wander around and see the sights."

"There are some beautiful spots in the city. And the beach is renowned."

"I didn't bring a bathing suit. Walking suits me."

He said nothing more and Rachel gazed at the scenery. It wouldn't be hard to drive from the village to Benidorm. So far the road ran straight along the sea. Anyone could manage.

It was more than a thirty-minute drive. Rachel couldn't stand the silence for that long.

"Tell me about growing olives," she said, hoping the topic would take the remainder of the car trip.

"What exactly do you wish to know?"

"All about the business. Do you sell olives, or press them for the oil? Are the olives harvested in fall? How is that done, by machine or by hand? Do you have your own refinery or do you just grow olives and sell? Why do it at all if you like writing?"

He glanced at her. "Growing olives has been the family business for generations. My father was actively involved, as were his father and grandfather. Now I run the business."

"Do you like that?"

"Not as much as writing."

"Then why do it?"

"It's the family concern. I was the only son, it is my duty to take charge. My sister has other interests."

"Obviously you still find time to write."

"As you say."

"So what do you do with the olives?"

For the rest of the ride, the discussion centered on how old some of the trees were, how they were harvested, what he looked for in the pressing process.

As Luis finished one reply, Rachel came up with another question. Some were quite basic, but he never commented on the fact, patiently answering each one. He never once made her feel foolish. Which was in direct contrast to Paul. The man thrived on pointing out his superior knowledge on everything he could think of.

Once they reached the large resort town of Benidorm, the traffic grew exponentially heavier. Luis dropped her near one of the main plazas, the old stone buildings a solid bulwark against time. She would be charmed if she had nothing better to do than wander around. But she wanted to find the library and get to business. Her tentative decision to begin groundwork to locate her mother had firmed into a strong resolve. Now she was impatient to get started.

She watched Luis drive away before she approached one of the *guardi* near the plaza's center to inquire after an Internet café. He directed her to one nearby and in only a few short moments, she was in line to use a computer. She sipped a *café con leche* while she waited, watching as others played games, or looked up information. Before too long, she was logged on and checking her own e-mail.

A letter waiting on her account from Caroline told Rachel of her father's attempts to locate her. Rachel responded, asking Caroline to assure her father she was fine, still angry and not ready yet to contact him herself. She couldn't help bragging to her friend about her job with writer J. L. Allen, swearing her to secrecy. She knew Caroline had read his books as well. She'd have to ask Luis if he'd autograph one for her friend.

Next she tried the name she was searching for, Loretta Goodson. Few results. She clicked on each one, but they didn't prove to be the woman she sought. If she couldn't turn up anything herself, eventually she'd try a private detective, someone who specialized in finding lost persons. She was determined to locate her mother if only to find out where she lived, what she was doing. The question of why she had not contacted her daughter in more than twenty years was something Rachel wasn't sure she wanted answered.

About to sign off, she hesitated. On impulse, she typed Luis's pseudonym into the search engine. A long list appeared. She clicked on the top one, reading about his last U.S. release, how the reviewers had loved it, how well sales had done.

Scanning the topics of the other articles on the list she stopped when she saw Bonita's name. Clicking on that article she found an American newspaper account of the tragedy. She didn't need the library after all. She'd be able to get all the information she wanted right here.

Quickly she skimmed the article. Luis was famous enough that anything surrounding him seemed newsworthy—especially the tragic death of his beloved wife.

The fateful night had been rainy. Bonita had been driving to visit someone and failed to negotiate one of the sharp curves on the road to the castle. She had plunged over the side, dying instantly. As had their unborn child.

Rachel stared at the article, unable to imagine the devastation and anguish Luis must have felt. Her heart ached for him. No wonder he mourned so many years later, he'd not only lost his beloved wife but the family they had started.

Esperenza was wrong. This just might be something he would never get over.

She clicked on another article, this one in Spanish. Reading the events, she was shocked further when it was suggested Luis had a hand in Bonita's death. Quickly she began reading closely from the beginning.

According to the article, he was never home, he neglected his duties in Spain, and denied his wife the attention she deserved. Instead of a grieving husband, this article painted a picture that almost accused him of murder!

CHAPTER FOUR

LUIS ADJUSTED HIS DARK glasses and leaned against the stone building. Readjusting the newspaper prop, he felt conspicuous and foolish. Hadn't he had his heros follow someone in more than one book? Never having actually tried it before, he didn't realize the many pitfalls—the most notable being what excuse would he give if Rachel saw him?

So far the surveillance had been boring. She'd gone to the *guardi*, asked a question, and been directed to a small café on a side street. She'd been inside for more than an hour. How much breakfast could she eat? What else was she doing in there? Had he missed the mark when he concluded she was not a reporter sent to get a story? Was she talking with a contact? Or had she arranged to meet someone to spend the day with? He was getting hot, but this corner was the best spot to watch the door without getting in anyone's way.

Impatiently he glanced at his watch. If she didn't show in another ten minutes, he'd move into the café himself and find out what she was doing.

Just then Rachel came out into the sunshine. She blinked at the brightness and quickly donned sunglasses. It made it more difficult to judge where she was looking, but he guessed he'd know immediately if she spotted him.

She sauntered down the street, gazing into store windows, studying displays. At the intersection, she waited for the traffic signal then crossed. Luis debated darting after her, but feared it would call attention. She didn't seem to be in a hurry, he could catch up after the next signal.

With no apparent destination in mind, Rachel wandered around the town. Luis grew impatient again. Was she just going to walk all day? She could have done that at home. The hills around the *castillo* had trails offering hikes of different degrees of difficulty. Or she could have explored the village. As to spending so much time in a café, Esperenza could have made her a dozen cups of coffee in the same length of time.

Close to noon, Rachel began to stop at restaurants and cafés, reading the posted menus.

"Enough," he said softly, moving to intercept.

"Rachel?" He hoped the surprise wasn't overdone. He'd never thought himself a very good actor. Though these last three years had proved that he could hide his feelings from family and friends.

"Luis? Are your offices nearby?"

"I thought I dropped you in another part of town." He didn't want to go into how far away the offices actually were. What excuse would he give if she pressed the issue?

"I've been walking around, seeing everything. The buildings are so old and intriguing. I wish I had a write-up of some. I bet they have fascinating histories."

"Have you had lunch?" he asked, not in the mood for a tour.

"Not yet."

"Join me," he said, slipping his hand around her elbow and guiding her toward the cross street. "There is a favorite restaurant of mine just a few blocks away."

"There's no need," she began, but he ignored her protest.

"I think you will like it. We'll have paella. Have you tried it?"

"Yes, when I first arrived in Andalucia. It's quite delicious."

"Carlos makes the best. Have you just been walking since I dropped you off?"

She shook her head. "I went first to an Internet café, to write to friends." Her expression was difficult to read. Was that guilt? Had she just been writing to friends, or filing a report?

"There is Internet access on my computer," he said, "No need to come to Benidorm.

"I checked, but didn't see a connection."

"Not the computer Maria uses. My laptop can be plugged into an outlet near the desk."

"Would it be all right if I use it sometimes?"

‘‘Of course. In fact, I often use it for research.’’ Had he not been holding her arm, he might not have noticed the slight tension radiating from her. Curious.

Had she been filing a report to some tabloid newspaper? If she used his computer, he could check the history log afterward to see if she was telling the truth. He wanted to trust her, beguiled by those eyes, no doubt. But he was an old hand at the games women played.

The restaurant was small and crowded. Luis spotted a table on the side and quickly headed for it. When they sat, their knees almost touched. He put his sunglasses on the table, and looked at Rachel. Her expression always seemed to be on the surface. Now she gazed around as if fascinated by the commotion and activity, but he suspected it was to avoid looking at him.

The tempting aromas from the kitchen focused their attention on food. Since he'd planned on paella, he didn't need the menu. Before long, they had cool glasses of wine before them, and the order placed.

She looked at him, a hint of wariness in her gaze. ‘‘Do you come here often?’’

‘‘Yes.’’

‘‘Is it near your offices?’’

‘‘No. I had…something else to do. Tell me how Spain compares with your home in California.’’

She shrugged. ‘‘There is no comparison. Here the buildings are old, made of stone and built to last. There’s history in every inch. Where I live in California, Malibu, it’s trendy, flashy and built to suit those who just moved in. People buy houses to tear them down and build new ones on the lots. I like Spain better.’’

‘‘So you came to vacation here?’’

‘‘I’ve wanted to for ages. The Romans, the Moors, even the Inquisition make it fascinating. And the architecture is so different as I said. Some of the cathedrals are wondrous to behold, even if they do need some dusting at the higher levels. The people are warm and friendly and not consumed with earning the almighty dollar.’’

"And people you know at home are consumed with earning the almighty dollar?"

She seemed to freeze. Then she slowly shook her head. "No, just a general statement."

"So what do you do when you are in California?"

"I work on charity events for the most part." She looked at him warily once again. "I really have done work as a secretary before, but never been paid."

He shrugged, trying to get a picture of her life before he met her. It sounded as if she came from money. But then, why the need of a job to stay in Spain? Couldn't she wire home for more funds?

Unless she was running away from something and couldn't access her own source of money.

Now that was something one of his heros would deduce. Was he seeing conspiracies where none existed? He'd have done better to pay attention to clues three years ago. He wouldn't make the same mistake twice.

"I'd rather hear how you got started writing thrillers for an American market when you live here, than talk about my boring life in California," she said.

"Before my father's death eight years ago, I spent a lot of time in the U.S. My parents separated when I was young. There was no divorce, but I spent most of the school year with my mother. Summers I spent here in Spain. I wrote my first book in the U.S., actually. After my father died and I inherited his estates, I moved here."

"But you come to the U.S. to do book tours and all, don't you?"

"I did for the earlier ones."

The paella arrived and they were silent for a while as they began to eat. He remembered the book tours with loathing. He did not like being friendly to total strangers who lined up to buy the books, then asked the most insane questions. He didn't like the way the men had ogled Bonita when she accompanied him. He hadn't liked her constant need for attention, and her urging him to do more with the media.

It all seemed so long ago. He had not been back to the States in the last three years. He didn't miss it.

Rachel wondered if Luis was thinking of his wife. How could that one article have suggested he had anything to do with her death? It was chilling to read the innuendoes of the Spanish newspaper. Nothing like it had been in the American versions. Had he seen those papers? Maybe he didn't even know the speculation that had run rampant.

She'd never met anyone connected with a violent death, much less a possible suspect for wrongdoing. Her curiosity level was off the charts, but she could not come up with a single way to find out the truth without asking him. And that she couldn't do.

She tried to imagine how she'd feel if she ever were so deeply in love and the person died. She'd be crushed. Life afterward must seem so much like just going through the motions. How tragic. Or was he not grieving, but hiding?

To take her mind off of the questions she might never get answered, she plunged into talk about California, surfing at the beach, skiing in the mountains and some of the excesses of its inhabitants. He seemed to listen, but she wondered once or twice if she were talking to herself.

"Did you enjoy the meal?" he asked when she put her fork down in completion.

The paella had been delicious and the wine just fruity and sweet enough to appeal to her. Rachel was full long before the paella pan was empty. Luis ate more than she, but even so there was enough left to feed another person or two.

"I enjoyed it very much. Thank you." Especially since her host had been most charming. Nothing like the taciturn man who had first opened his door to her a few days ago. Nothing like a man who might have wished harm to his beautiful wife.

Learning what she had about her employer from the Internet articles, she felt she had known him much longer. It came from discovering some of the most intimate parts of his life. In a normal growth of friendship, such information might be a long time being shared.

Yet he knew very little about her. Not that her life was the open book she had once thought it.

"The pleasure was mine, Rachel. I enjoyed learning more about California," he said.

"Did you ever visit?"

"San Francisco and Los Angeles on one book tour. It rained in San Francisco and was hot even in November in Los Angeles. I think I'd prefer the southern California climate."

"It's nice. Temperate like here."

"If you are finished, may I escort you to your next stop?"

"Actually I've pretty much done all I needed to do. Have you finished your business?"

"Yes." He paid the bill and rose, gesturing for her to lead the way. Reaching the sidewalk, he once again donned his dark glasses. Rachel wished she could still see his eyes. The lighting in the restaurant had been a bit dim, and now it was too bright to be without sunglasses.

She put her own on and looked around. "Is your car nearby?"

"No, it's in a lot a few blocks away. We'll get a taxi."

"Or walk, if it's not too far. I love ambling along and looking at everything. Unless you're in a hurry?"

"I'm in no hurry."

As they strolled along the wide sidewalks, Rachel peered into the various display windows trying to decide if Luis could have done something so horrendous as was hinted at in that article.

Drat, she wished she'd never read the thing. Now she couldn't forget it. Every step she was conscious of Luis beside her. He'd been more attentive today than ever. Was he looking for friendship? Had he just been in a bad mood earlier and this was more like his normal personality?

She wondered if she could resist this new personality. He had made her aware of him and her own feelings before. Now she was afraid she wouldn't find the determination to resist.

* * *

The next several days flew by. Rachel faithfully continued transcribing the manuscript pages. She'd read the opening and found herself torn between trying to guess what was coming next, and trying to figure out if Luis had had something to do with his wife's accident.

According to Esperenza, he had been heartbroken at his wife's death. Was that report in the newspaper merely one man's attempt to sell more papers?

When she had finished working each day, she'd used the Internet access he'd given to comb the Web for information on Loretta Goodson. Inevitably she would end up each day reading more about Luis Alvares, or J. L. Allan as he was known in the press. She had not found anything new about the tragedy with Bonita, but she'd learned a lot about the woman from articles of happier times. Her pictures showed a sultry brunette who liked expensive clothes and bright colors. Her smile was provocative, sexy. Her exploits were notorious. She obviously liked fast living. How had she liked the *castillo* and its relative isolation?

Rachel grew depressed reading about her. She seemed to have it all. Including Luis's devotion. What had really happened that rainy night three years ago?

"If you wish information concerning my private life, you should have asked me," Luis said from behind her. Anger laced his tone as he reached over and disconnected the Internet connection.

Rachel froze, her eyes still on another article about Bonita's death. She had not heard him. He was home early. And, of course, if he'd used the door from the hall instead of the French doors, she'd have had enough warning to clear the screen.

There was no denying what she was reading. She turned slightly and looked up at him. "I was curious."

"And that gives you the right to pry into my affairs?"

"Hardly prying if it's on the Internet for the entire world to see. But I can see your point." She pushed back her chair and stood, putting some distance between them. "Um, if I had asked you any questions, wouldn't you have thought me some kind of reporter? I distinctly remember you thinking that the first day."

"Are you?"

"Oh, for goodness' sakes, no! You can't tell? I'm reading articles to find out more about you. Not to write about you."

"You could be doing background research so you don't cover the same ground in your own articles."

"Or I could be just who I am, someone who is low on money and needed a job to tide me over."

"Why not wire home for more money?" he asked.

Rachel's mind went blank. What had she already told him about her family? Had she mentioned her father?

"I want to stand on my own two feet."

"And how is it you planned this vacation and didn't allow for the money you'd need. When do you return to the States?"

"Things turned out to be more expensive. And I'll leave when I'm ready. But not before Maria returns. You need me."

"I have managed all this time without you," he said.

"What about the fiesta tonight?" she countered triumphantly. He wouldn't fire her for being curious, would he?

"Point to you. But in future, I would appreciate your asking me if you have questions, not researching other people's ideas of what happened."

"Did you sue?" she asked suddenly.

"What?"

"There is one terrible article that suggests you might have had something to do with the accident. Did you sue them for slander?"

"Actually it would have been libel, had they been more blunt. But, no, I did not sue. They are entitled to their slant on the news."

"You didn't have anything to do with it, did you?"

"What do you think?"

Rachel let her instincts guide her. "No."

"A vote of confidence I didn't expect. As it happens, you are only partly right. I did not tamper with her car, but we had a flaming row and she left in a temper. I've always wondered if that had anything to do with her driving skills that night."

"That's awful. How horrible for you, remembering that. But I thought it was raining. It was stormy, surely that contributed to the accident."

He shocked her when he said, "It's not as horrible as you might imagine. Of course, that was because of the topic of the fight."

"What was it?"

"That, Miss Nosy, is none of your business, nor anyone else's. And you won't find it in any newspaper account, either."

"I'm sorry for your loss, nonetheless," she said.

"She was a beautiful woman," he said slowly, staring at the small photo on the computer screen. "She died too young." He looked at Rachel again. "This is how you use the Internet?"

"No, actually, I'm searching for my mother."

"Your mother?" He looked startled. "Is she lost?"

"Apparently. To me anyway. I recently discovered she was not dead as I'd always thought, but had been driven from home when I was a small child." Actually she had no knowledge of why her mother had left. But being forced to leave her child sounded better to Rachel than to think the woman had just left with no problem or regrets.

"Driven from home? By whom?"

"My father, I think," she replied flatly.

She could almost see the connection clicking in his mind.

"Recently discovered as in just prior to this trip?"

She nodded.

"So you don't send home for more money because it would mean taking it from your father?"

"I don't send home for money because I don't want him to know where I am."

"Ah. That explains a great deal."

She stared at him, wondering if he planned to use that information in a way she wouldn't appreciate. But he still didn't know who her father was, or how to contact him. Her hiding place was safe a little longer.

Or was it? He had her passport with her address. Would he use it to contact her father?

"Where do we go from here?" she asked.

He stepped closer, crowding her space. "I won't pursue your father if you drop the research on my private life," Luis said.

"Deal," she said quickly, holding out her hand. His story was in the past, but she was living hers now. And she needed more time to gather her defenses against her father and Paul.

He took her hand in his. Rachel wasn't expecting the heat that seemed to engulf her with his touch. She stared at him, wondering if he was casting some kind of spell.

But he didn't seem to notice anything amiss and after a brief shake, released her.

Rachel would have agreed to anything to save him notifying her father of where she was. But the commitment didn't end her curiosity. She just wished she'd found out a bit more about him before agreeing to stop her own research into his past.

"Tonight is the fiesta. The village is already filling up with tourists and family members who have come to celebrate. There will be plenty to eat there, so I gave Esperenza the evening off. We'll leave at five, instead of seven as I originally said."

That explained why he was home early.

"I'll be ready." She wished now that she hadn't committed to going.

"We'll circulate a little, I'll give my this-is-a-good-year speech and we'll leave."

"I'll do my best to keep the groupies away."

"That should prove interesting."

When they arrived in the village for the fiesta, Rachel was amazed at how it had been transformed from the last time she'd seen it. The crowds were surprising, even though Luis had warned her. The colorful lights strung everywhere would be especially delightful after dark. Flowers bedecked every surface, and there were vendor booths at every corner, selling flowers, trinkets and food.

The mood was festive. People laughed and danced in the street.

Not, of course, Luis.

He grew more grim and taciturn the closer they drew to the village. By the time he'd parked the car several blocks from the center of town, he was scowling.

"Let's get this over with," he muttered, gesturing her to precede him along the crowded sidewalk. "The speaker's stand will be in the square."

The party mood was contagious. Rachel smiled at the friendly greetings, feeling the excitement and happiness from everyone. Luis remained silent, walking steadily toward the center as if his life depended upon reaching it without speaking a word.

"Luis!" An exuberant young woman stopped in front of him, forcing him to a halt. She flung her arms around his neck and kissed him on the mouth.

Rachel looked on, startled. Obviously a good friend. Why hadn't he invited her to the fiesta?

Luis pulled her arms down and held her away from him. ''Rosalie,'' he said.

''I didn't expect you. Juan didn't say you were coming. How are you, *querido*? You never return my calls. You can't be that busy!''

''Things have been hectic since Maria was injured.''

''I would be happy to help out, you know that.''

Her dark eyes were beautiful, as was the rest of her, Rachel thought. Her own blond coloring looked faint and insipid beside the lush beauty.

Luis looked at her. Rachel wondered if he was reading her mind.

''Rachel, may I present Rosalie Fontana. Rosalie, this is Rachel Goodson. A...a friend.''

Rachel smiled politely, which was more than Rosalie did. She glanced at Rachel, then back to Luis, suspicion in every inch.

"A friend? I have not met her before."

"Rachel's visiting from America," he replied, reaching out to take Rachel's arm and draw her close.

So the games begin, she thought, trying to figure out what he wanted. Were they to pretend she and Luis had embarked on a passionate love affair to keep away the matchmakers? She leaned slightly against him and smiled. "It's so nice to meet a friend of Luis," she said.

Rosalie made no effort to even be polite.

"When did you arrive?"

"A week or so ago," Rachel replied.

Rosalie frowned. "I heard nothing of a guest arriving from Sophia."

"And she would need to inform you because why?" Luis asked.

Rachel wondered who Sophia was, but didn't ask. If she was someone close to Luis, Rachel should probably already know that. The best way to succeed in this charade was to say as little as possible. And snuggle up to her stern boss with all evidence of enjoyment.

"Of course she would not need to inform me, but I saw her for lunch last week and she made no mention of your having a guest."

"My sister does not know everything. Is she here today?"

"She's coming later." Rosalie put her hand on Luis's arm. "I'm delighted to see you. Maybe later you will dance with me."

Luis inclined his head, but made no further commitment.

"You will excuse us, I need to find Juan," he said, drawing Rachel away as if she wanted to linger and he had no time.

"See you again," Rachel called over her shoulder, just to provoke the woman.

Her glare was what Rachel expected.

"Sophia is your sister?" Rachel asked quietly when they were half a block along.

"*Si.* She lives in Benidorm. She and Rosalie have been close friends for years."

"And which one wants Rosalie for you?" she asked.

He glanced at her. "Picked up on that, did you?"

"It was too obvious. Why not call her to accompany you tonight?"

"I do not wish to give rise to false hopes. I have no interest in Rosalie."

"So tell your sister."

"I have done so on more than one occasion. But she sees no evidence of my interest in any other direction, so believes persistence will pay off."

"So I'm to fool your sister as well?"

"A minor diversion to get her off my back. She is the worst of the matchmakers."

"Somehow I don't see you putting up with anything like a pesky sister," Rachel said dryly.

"We all have our crosses to bear. Ah, there is Juan."

They had reached the town square. At the center was a raised platform with two rows of chairs. A podium and microphone were already in place. A colorful canopy sheltered the platform from the late afternoon sun. Sprays of flowers surrounded the base so it appeared to be floating on blossoms.

Luis introduced her to Juan. The two men discussed the program and the crowd. They would not start the speeches until after seven.

Luis didn't look happy, but he said nothing except that they would return in time. Rachel wondered what they would do for the next couple of hours.

He looked around the crowded square acknowledging several people who called greetings. Though they looked curiously at Rachel, he didn't stop to talk with them or introduce her.

"If we have two hours, let's wander around and see the booths. I've never seen a fiesta before. What is this celebrating?" Rachel asked.

"It's in honor of our patron saint. The village likes any excuse to have fiesta. There are several during the year."

"Don't you like them?" Rachel asked. How could anyone keep such a somber face in such delightful surroundings?

"Not anymore. Come, there is someone I wish to speak to."

In only a moment, Luis had introduced her to Pablo and Maria Sanchez. Pablo was a foreman overseeing the olive groves Luis owned. It was obvious the two men were friends as well.

"So you come to the fiesta at last," Pablo said after introductions were made. "I hope you enjoy the evening," he said to Rachel.

"I'm having a great time so far," she murmured. She liked both him and his wife.

Luis had not had a single person visit in the nine days she'd been in residence. Except for the maids, Esperenza and the gardener she'd glimpsed at a distance, there was no one at the *castillo* but Luis and herself.

Had he cut himself off entirely from friends after Bonita's death? Or had they believed the innuendoes published in those articles and stayed away for fear he had had a hand in the accident? How awful if his friends had not stood by him.

"Luis!" A petite young woman quickly crossed the road and hurried over to the small group. "Luis, I didn't know you were planning to attend." She gave him a quick hug and then smiled at Pablo and Maria. ''Hello. I might have known Luis would be with you two if he showed up.'' She turned back to Luis. ''Why didn't you tell me you were coming? Julian and the baby are over there saving me a seat. We would have saved you one as well.''

''We're sitting on the dias, as it happens,'' he said.

''We?'' She looked at Pablo.

''Rachel and I. Sophia, may I present Rachel Goodson, a friend visiting from America.''

Rachel was surprised he wanted to maintain the charade with his family, but saw it as necessary to keep Rosalie at bay. She had never had a sibling. Did they all interfere with each other's lives?

''Hello.'' She wished she could say more, but the stunned look on Sophia's face stopped her.

''You are visiting Luis?'' Sophia asked.

Rachel nodded.

She looked at her brother. ''A friend from America?''

Luis reached for Rachel's hand and kissed the back briefly. "A very dear friend, come to stay for a few weeks."

"How surprising." She smiled politely at Rachel. "Forgive me, this has caught me by surprise. I didn't know Luis was expecting a visitor. He made no mention of it the last time I saw him."

"My arrival was unexpected," Rachel said.

"You two will have to come to dinner tomorrow night. I want to get to know you better. But for now, come meet my husband. I know Julian will want to meet you as well. And you can see my baby. Mario is the perfect infant."

"So speaks a doting mother," Luis said.

She threw him a look, and continued, "The fiesta is not the place to sit and chat. Tomorrow we can get to know each other better."

"We have plans for tomorrow," Luis said quickly.

"Oh? Then the next evening," Sophia said, not to be stopped.

"I'll call you when we get home tonight."

"You are staying at the *castillo*?" Sophia asked Rachel.

She nodded, glancing at Luis. He probably planned to explain everything when he spoke with his sister later. It was hard to explain his strategy with Pablo and Marie standing by.

"I for one am happy her visit coincided with fiesta. I think Luis might not have come otherwise, eh, friend?" Pablo said.

"Showing Rachel around was certainly one incentive to come."

"Oh, no, you're not doing the man of the castle speech, are you?" Sophia said. She looked at Rachel. "Did he tell you? Our father always gave the speech, almost verbatim every year. It was part of the tradition of the fiesta, but we used to hate to attend. We could have quoted him perfectly."

"I plan to do so tonight," Luis said. The amusement lurking in his eyes clued Rachel in to his joke. Sophia didn't look amused. "You better find close seats when we gather on the dias so you don't miss a word," he added. "Pablo, I'll call you next week."

Rachel's hand was still clasped in his as they walked away to meet Sophia's husband and baby. As soon as was polite, Luis made an excuse and they left, strolling through the crowd.

"Doing it a bit thick, don't you think?" She held up their linked hands. "Don't you plan to clue in your sister at all?" Rachel asked when they were far enough away to not be overheard.

"And have her tell Rosalie? Not on your life. A couple of pertinent demonstrations will go a long way to making my life less complicated."

"Well, that's sure my goal, make your life less complicated," she murmured.

"Good." Ignoring the curious glances of others, he leaned over to kiss her on the mouth.

CHAPTER FIVE

IT WAS A BRIEF BRUSH of lips, but it shocked Rachel. She blinked. "What was that for?"

"To mark my claim?" he said. "Let Sophia, Rosalie and anyone else interested know I'm not on the market."

"Oh."

They continued to wander the streets. Luis bought her food from one stand, a drink from another. At a third, he bought her a bright fan, which she promptly opened and used. Peering at him over the edge, she smiled. "The Southerners used to use fans to great advantage when flirting," she said.

He looked at her. "And are you flirting with me?"

"Shouldn't I? If we want to fool anyone who was looking," she said, batting her eyes at him.

"I can see why it's so effective. Only your expressive eyes are showing."

Expressive eyes? She blinked. It almost sounded like a compliment.

Luis laughed, reaching out to lower the fan. "Don't ever play poker, you'll lose your shirt."

Luis insisted Rachel accompany him on the platform when it was time. She was conscious of hundreds of eyes watching her every move. In for a penny, she thought and turned to smile at Luis. "I'm having such a wonderful time," she said, letting her fingers walk up his arm. "Can I put this on my résumé?"

He leaned closer, bringing his lips close to her ear. "You are playing the part so well. I'm not sure where it falls on a résumé, but I'll give a glowing recommendation. Shall we stay for the dance?"

"I would love to, will that be before or after the fireworks?" More pretense?

"Dancing starts before the fireworks, but goes on until the last person drops—usually just before dawn."

She gazed at him, their faces so close they almost touched. To anyone watching, it would look like an intimate lovers' discussion. Her heart caught, then began to beat more rapidly. It was only make-believe. But for an instant, she wondered what it would be like to have him genuinely interested in her. She expected it would be like nothing she'd ever known before.

The spell was broken when Juan began to fiddle with the microphone. The loud squeals and static caught people's attention instantly.

Rachel had been behind the scenes on many events such as this, and knew how it would likely unfold. The speeches were short and entertaining. When Luis spoke, however, if she had closed her eyes, she would not have known it was him. He held the crowd spellbound. He made them laugh, had them cheering. He was obviously held in high regard, and his neighbors had missed him at recent fiestas.

When the official program ended, people swarmed the stairs to greet Luis. He spoke to each, introducing Rachel again and again. She smiled until her cheeks ached, knowing she would never remember most of the names, but hoping she was playing the role of devoted *friend.*

Darkness fell as they were talking and the string of lights came on everywhere, making the village appear like a fairyland.

When the music started, Luis swept her onto the dance floor and held her close.

"I didn't see any groupies," she mentioned. She felt like an enchanted princess waiting for the stroke of twelve. This was all fantasy, but she was savoring every moment.

"Ah, your presence worked."

"Most of the people seem to associate you with the olive groves, not writing. They do know you're an author, don't they?"

"Some do. The books are not as popular here as in the United States. I don't make a big deal of it and the name is unfamiliar, of course." He shrugged. "Here, I'm just the son of Juan Baptist Alvares. It suits me."

When the music ended, Rosalie popped up beside them. "Our dance, Luis?"

He looked at her and shook his head. "Tonight is for Rachel. Another time." He drew Rachel closer, his arm around her waist.

Rosalie obviously disliked his response, but tossed her head and looked around for someone else.

The next song was a slow one. Luis drew Rachel into his arms and moved with the dreamy rhythm.

Every cell in her body knew she was pressed against him. Her blood heated in her veins. Her heart rate tripled, and she had trouble breathing.

When his lips brushed against her temple, she almost stumbled. Anyone watching, and she didn't doubt a lot of people were watching, would suspect they were lovers. That was his intent, wasn't it?

"So, you have moved on." A harsh male voice interrupted her thoughts. Luis stopped dancing, dropped his arms and turned to face the man.

"Jose."

"So quickly you forget Bonita." He glanced at Rachel and dismissed her.

"I have not forgotten Bonita," Luis said quietly. "She will always be with me."

"She loved fiesta."

Luis nodded, his eyes hooded, his expression impassive.

"This one will never bring you the passion Bonita had."

"It's the blond hair," Rachel said, tired of the dirty looks.

"What?" Jose looked startled.

"A lot of people think blondes are cool and collected. But we have just as much passion as anyone. Right, Luis?"

"I have no complaints," he said softly, his amused gaze on her.

"Then maybe we should return home," she said as provocatively as she could manage. Let Jose think on that!

"Do you really wish to leave? The fireworks will be starting soon."

"We can watch them from our special place."

"*A dios*, Jose." Luis led the way back to the car without another word.

Once inside, he looked at her. "Our special place?"

She grinned. "Sounded good, don't you think? I meant on the old wall, where you said you used to watch the fireworks. Unless you and Bonita watched them there and they'd hold sad memories.

"No, usually Bonita and I attended the fiesta together. It was when I was younger that I watched fireworks from the wall. I thought you'd want to stay longer."

"Why? To fight with Rosalie? Be interrupted by irrate men. What's the story with Jose, anyway? An admirer of your wife?"

"Maybe." He started the car and began the drive to the castle.

"Maybe? What does that mean?"

"Drop the subject. I told you, no more questions about my past."

So much for the feeling of camaraderie she had begun to feel around him. Firmly put in her place, she refused to speak again until they reached the castle.

Once there, she quickly got out of the car and looked at him over the roof. "Thank you for taking me, I hope I provided services as required," she said stiffly.

"Services rendered were more than satisfactory."

"Good." She slammed the car door and headed for the castle. She'd get her flashlight and head for the wall to see the fireworks. Alone.

"Where are you going?"

"To get a flashlight."

"We don't need a flashlight, I know the way perfectly well."

She hesitated. "No need to continue the charade. I'll watch them, you can go brood in your lair."

"My lair?"

She wisely kept quiet.

"Come watch the fireworks with me—from our special place," he said softly.

She headed back. "You know that was for show. If you have something else you'd rather do—"

"I don't." He took her hand as they walked away from the castle. "To keep you from getting off the path," he explained.

She didn't need any explanation. What she needed was some distance from the disturbing man. But he held her hand firmly and led the way to the wall.

Rachel sat gingerly on the still-warm stones, swinging her legs over and studying the pretty scene laid out before them. They had hardly settled before the first burst of color lit up the night.

"*Ohhh,*" she said in delight.

"I imagine I'll hear *ooh* and *ahh* all through the display," he murmured dryly. "I remember that from the one Independence Day Celebration we spent in the States. Usually Sophia and I spent the summers here, but one year my American grandparents insisted we spend the early part of July with them."

"Only one?"

"Summers were the only time I had to spend with my father until I was out of school."

She nodded, watching as another burst of color filled the night sky. "These are worth exclaiming over. I love fireworks."

She gazed in delight as the festive display continued for several minutes. The big finale was dazzling. When it ended, she sighed happily.

''I'm surprised such a small village could afford such a lavish display,'' she commented, swiveling around to stand on the ground again.

Luis was beside her. Too close. She looked up, but couldn't see him clearly, only his silhouette against the star-studded sky.

''The village has a fund people contribute to all year. Our company makes up any shortfall.''

''Oh.'' She couldn't think. He was too close.

''Rachel.'' He said her name softly, his hand coming to brush against her hair. ''Like silk,'' he said softly. ''Tell me. Do you think a man should mourn the loss of his wife forever?''

''N-no. Life goes on.'' She cleared her throat, nerves taut with anticipation.

''For some it seems to move slowly.'' He leaned closer, blotting out the stars.

His lips covered hers in a warm kiss.

Rachel closed her eyes to better savor the sensations that began to fill her. His mouth moved gently, coaxing a response she could no more deny than she could fly.

When his arms drew her close against his body, she put her arms around his neck and returned his kiss with enthusiasm.

The fireworks she'd just seen were nothing in comparison to the splash of wild color behind her eyelids. She felt more alive than ever in her life. Yet there was more, she just knew it.

When Luis ended the kiss, she wanted to cry out. It was too soon.

He rested his head against her forehead. "Is there a man back in California awaiting your return from vacation?" he asked.

"There is no one," she whispered, moving closer, wanting another kiss.

He must have read her mind because he kissed her again, his lips opening her. His tongue touched hers lightly, then danced against hers, as if enticing her into further intimacies.

The sensations that grew threatened to overwhelm Rachel, but she wouldn't exchange one moment in time for this one. She only wished they could go on forever.

"I want you, Rachel," he said, moving to kiss her cheeks, trailing little kisses to her throat. He settled his mouth on the pounding pulse point and lingered.

His words were like a glass of cold water thrown into her face. She stopped responding, and pulled away.

"Let's not let this charade get out of control. We're pretending involvement to keep the groupies away, remember?"

"Ah, was that the reason for your passionate kiss? I was under the impression it was to make sure I knew your assertion to Jose was accurate."

"Why did you kiss me to begin with?"

"I just told you, I want you."

Her heart pounding, she stared at him, wishing she could see him in the darkness.

"This is just make-believe," she repeated, to convince him or for herself, she wasn't sure.

"What if we want to change the rules, for as long as you are here?"

"What do you mean?" she whispered.

"A summer affair?"

Her heart pounded. No one had ever suggested she have an affair with them. Two men had wanted to marry her—for closer connections with her father. And Paul, of course. But even he had never pretended a passion that wasn't there.

This was outside her realm of experience. Was Luis serious? She wasn't the kind of woman with whom men had passionate affairs.

"I need time to think about it," she said. What was there to think about? She had left California to escape overbearing men. She had no reason to think Luis was any different. And she certainly had not fled one problem to become entangled with another.

Yet—the undeniable appeal was there. The man was fascinating. His kisses set her aflame. She wanted to know more about him, and about where such kisses led. Spend time with him and erase the sadness of loss. Explore the joy of involvement.

"Do not take too long," he said, and turned to walk away.

Rachel watched until she could no longer make him out in the darkness. Fortunately her eyes had adjusted to the lack of light so she could make her way back to the castle without straying from the path. She concentrated on walking, refusing to think about her feelings at the moment. A total jumble of conflicting thoughts best described her mind at the moment.

But once she reached her room, Luis's words echoed again and again. She fell into bed thinking about what it would be like to spend time with him. Share kisses, caresses. She opened her eyes wide in startled awareness. It wouldn't only be kisses. He actually wanted to make love to her.

"Oh, wow," she said softly.

"Oh, no," she said in dismay.

Rachel entered the study the next morning expecting to see Luis. He had not been in the kitchen, having eaten much earlier according to Esperanza. He wasn't in the room. As late as it was, he had probably long left for Benidorm. She bet he was bright-eyed and ready to tackle any problem that came along.

She had tossed and turned all night, alternating with finding his comments wildly romantic, and being suspicious of why he'd picked her out. Rosalie would have been more than willing, she knew. There were several lovely women he'd introduced her to last night. Why her?

After a nonproductive morning, Rachel ate a quick lunch and then headed up the path to the gazebo. She needed some clear thinking. Feeling the pull of attraction to Luis in the castle even with him gone, she hoped expanding her horizons, if only visually, would help her sort her jumbled thoughts.

The view was wondrous. But did nothing to aid her decision.

Fact one—she was majorly attracted to Luis Alvares. There was no denying that. And she couldn't see it going anywhere.

Fact two—he was as dynamic as her father, Paul and a dozen other men she knew. Extremely successful business types tended to be driven and hard and focused.

Fact three—there was no meeting of the minds. She was still learning about him. Most of the days she'd been here, he'd been suspicious. That had eased—or had it? Was this some convoluted ploy on his part in hopes she'd confess?

Fact four—she'd never had an affair. This was probably the largest stumbling block. What would it be like? Was he only after her compliance in bed, or would it mean spending their free time together? Exploring more about each other, sharing thoughts and feelings?

Somehow she didn't see Luis as the touchy-feely kind of guy interested in sharing any *feelings.* She saw him more as the full-speed-ahead kind of man, going after what he wanted with determination. He had to have enormous willpower and control to be able to run a huge company and find time to write books that sold so well.

Did she want that focus on her?

Being romanced by a dashing Spaniard, wined and dined in fancy restaurants, romantic dancing until dawn sounded great in theory. She just wasn't sure this was the time or place to so indulge.

She was attracted to the man. Could she keep her emotions firmly in check and explore all an affair would offer? Or would she end up falling for him, even knowing going in that there was no future.

"So have you decided?"

He stood in the arch of the gazebo, dressed in black slacks and a white shirt. The collar was opened at the throat, revealing a strong brown neck. She studied him for several moments, letting the awareness build, testing her own strength against the yearning that built.

"Yes," she replied.

The sudden flare in his eyes surprised her.

"No."

"What?" he asked, crossing to stand in front of her. Rachel could feel the heat from his body as it radiated outward and engulfed her.

"I mean, yes I've decided, and I have to say no. Thank you," she added.

For an instant she thought he looked disappointed, but that was ridiculous. Nothing would faze Luis.

He raised his hand slowly and softly touched her hair, letting the strands wrap around his fingers. "Is it you don't feel the same attraction I feel?"

Her heart rate tripled. Had the air vanished? She was having trouble breathing.

"Don't you want more than just some sexual attraction?"

"Like what?" He leaned closer, lowering his head, his mouth coming closer.

"I don't know…"

She trailed off as he brushed his lips against her once, twice. Then he wrapped his arms around her and pulled her against him as he kissed her.

His lips moved over hers, teasing, coaxing. When she parted her lips, he didn't take advantage instantly, but continued the sweet coaxing until she relaxed and returned his pressure. When his tongue swept against her lips, she tentatively reacted with her own, to touch and taste. Every inch of her was alive as she'd never been before. She could kiss and be kissed by Luis forever.

He didn't push for more, seemingly content with their kiss. Others had always gone faster than she had wanted at this stage and so often Rachel had ended up fighting off unwelcomed advances. Had he pursued it, Rachel doubted she'd resist.

When he ended the kiss, she slowly opened her eyes to find him staring down at her.

"Reconsider," he said softly.

"I'd think you'd want more than just sex," she said with some asperity as she disentangled herself from him and put several feet of much needed space between them. How was she supposed to even think with her mind still numb from his kisses?

"Like what?"

"Like what you had with your wife," she snapped. Her mood was fast deteriorating. She had thought things through and decided to refuse. Now after one kiss, she was reconsidering just as he'd probably known she would.

He looked as if she'd slapped him.

"Don't be confusing yourself with my wife," he said.

"I'm not. I just mean if sex is all you want, find it elsewhere. If I make love with someone, I want it to mean more than just a romp between the sheets. I want caring and respect and…"

She stopped abruptly. She was not looking for love from Luis Alvares. If she said it, he'd immediately think she was after more than what he offered.

"And?" he asked dangerously.

"And, and…something in common. We have none of that. You suspect I'm some kind of spy. I don't know you except as the man who hired me to type a manuscript."

"You've read my books. Surely you have some kind of feeling about what kind of man I am."

"Dutiful, honorable, focused, and successful," she said after a moment. "Those are traits. I still don't know you."

"I don't know you well, either, but I'm willing to take a chance. You could still be a tabloid reporter, biding her time. Or someone who wants marriage and is being very clever."

"What if I'm just who I say I am. Someone on vacation in Spain?"

"Who doesn't call home for money when she runs out. Who claims she has no man waiting for her, but I find that hard to believe."

"Why?"

He stepped closer. Rachel held her ground, watching him warily.

"You have the passion you told Jose about. You are beautiful. I know American men are not blind."

He was crowding her space. She longed to turn and flee, but she was held in place by the intensity of his gaze, by the melodious sound of his voice, the words that flattered beyond any she'd ever heard before. He thought she was beautiful? Passionate?

"Well, maybe," she temporized.

"Maybe there is a man?" he asked.

"No, maybe I'll consider an affair. But only after I get to know you better. And you me."

He cupped her chin in his hand and tilted up her face. "How long?"

"Well for goodness' sakes, Luis, I don't know. There isn't a timetable. When it's right, I guess."

"And until then?"

She licked her lips when his gaze moved to watch her tongue. The desire was so strong she could almost touch it.

"We get to know each other?" she asked softly.

"We'll try it your way for a few days. I'm not a patient man." He lowered his head and kissed her.

"Señor?" A voice came from a small speaker in the gazebo that Rachel had not even noticed.

Luis broke the kiss and hurried to the post, pressing a small button. *"Si?"*

"Your sister is most insistent she talk to you," Esperenza said.

"I'll be there in a moment." He looked at Rachel. "Until later." Quickly he strode from the structure.

Rachel watched him, bemused. Until later? What did that mean? It almost sounded like an ultimatum. He planned to try it her way for a few days. At the end, what? Would they re-evaluate the situation, or was he expecting her compliance at the end of a few days?

Would she be able to resist? If he applied himself to seducing her, she had a feeling she would be more than willing to go along with whatever he planned.

So much for clearing her head by coming up to the gazebo, she thought wryly. She was more muddled after those fabulous kisses than she'd ever been.

Rachel didn't see Luis again that evening. When she arrived at the patio for dinner, Esperenza was the only one there, placing the platter of pork in the center of the table.

"Señor Alvares had to go back to Benidorm for business. He sends his apologies," she said as she surveyed the table with satisfaction.

"Nothing crucial, I hope," Rachel murmured as she sat.

Esperenza shrugged.

"Will you join me?" Rachel asked, not wishing to eat in solitary splendor.

"I have already eaten," the older woman replied.

"It looks delicious."

"Señor Luis had a call from his sister. She phoned earlier, before the business matter. She asked about you."

Rachel was tempted to tell her she'd known about Sophia's call, but didn't wish to have to explain how. Merely nodding, she began to eat. The evening hadn't turned out like she'd hoped. Had Luis gone to his sister's? Or had work demanded his attention?

Luis drove home rapidly. He had been needed at the consortium's office to deal with a problem. The timing, in his opinion, couldn't have been worse. He had made definite strides in persuading Rachel to indulge in an affair with him. Had he lost ground by being absent this evening? Would she still be awake, wanting to learn more about him, to justify her compliance?

Women played strange games. He wanted her, she wanted him, what was the difference if they waited until they knew each other's school grades or grandparents' names? He wasn't looking for a lifelong commitment. He'd tried that once and look where it had gotten him.

Rachel wasn't moving to Spain, only visiting. It was perfect. With the added bonus of keeping others at bay. Most noticeably Rosalie. Not that invitations had been lacking in the last three years. Women especially seemed to think a man alone, a widower, needed a woman in his life.

As he rounded one of the bends in the road and saw the castle, he acknowledged someday he would probably feel the need to find another wife in order to have a child to inherit the family home. Or, maybe he'd settle for Sophia's children inheriting. They weren't a dynasty from ancient times. Luis wasn't sure he'd ever again trust a woman enough to marry her.

The castle appeared in darkness when he drew into the courtyard. No lights shone from the windows. Esperenza had left the carriage lights on, but nothing else. In other words, Rachel's window was dark. Damn.

Unless she hadn't yet gone up. Maybe she was in the lounge or the study. He'd check both before retiring.

She was in neither. But her scent seemed to linger in the air of the study, even with the French doors opened to the evening's breeze. Imagination or reality? He was growing fanciful as he aged, he mocked himself. The night air was redolent with scents from nearby blossoms. That was what he smelled, not Rachel's perfume.

He refused to admit disappointment she hadn't waited for him. If he took her at her word, he'd believe she wasn't as interested as he.

Saturday morning Luis awoke early. Day one in his new campaign.

By the time he reached the kitchen, he'd formulated his strategy.

Rachel was talking with Esperenza as the housekeeper prepared coffee. They both looked at him when he entered, surprise and speculation in Esperenza's gaze, wariness in Rachel's.

"Good morning, Señor. I shall have breakfast ready soon."

"No rush. I'll join you both in here if I may," he said, taking a chair opposite to Rachel. "Sleep well?" he asked Rachel.

"Yes."

"Today we can go to the beach," Luis said, ignoring the wariness in her eyes. "It seems a shame to come all the way to the Mediterranean and not take advantage of all it offers."

Her smile lit up her face. Luis felt it as if he'd been punched. He wanted to sweep her upstairs into his room, close the door and stay in bed all day. She was not a sultry beauty like Bonita had been. Her blondness belied the passion she'd bragged about to Jose, and he was determined to tap into it as soon as possible.

"I would love to get to the beach. If you could drop me there, that would be terrific. I was thinking that very thing earlier."

"I told her to ask you for your mother's car," Esperenza interjected.

Luis frowned. It was not his intention to make things easier for Rachel to do things without him. ‘‘The car needs to be serviced first.’’ He’d see it stayed in the shop for several days.

Esperenza merely raised an eyebrow in disbelief, but said nothing.

‘‘I meant we’d go together. I like to swim,’’ Luis said smoothly.

‘‘That would be great,’’ Rachel said, color staining her cheeks.

He wished he could read her mind. Her enthusiasm had dipped when he said he’d accompany her. But her eyes held hidden promise.

Whatever her true feelings, he looked forward to the excursion. It would provide her with the chance to grow more comfortable around him, and give him a chance to push for more. Timing was everything, as he’d learned in the past. Now to turn it to his advantage.

CHAPTER SIX

RACHEL STUDIED HERSELF in the mirror, hoping the bikini she wore wasn't too blatant. It was the only suit she'd brought. And she hadn't used it once since she arrived in Spain. She tried to imagine how Luis would like it.

Not that it mattered, she told herself, but she suspected he would like it a lot. Smiling, she turned to don the coverup and slip into sandals. She didn't want to keep him waiting. Nor keep herself in suspense as to the reason for his invitation. Was it to get to know her better, or try an inquisition? Weren't the Spanish famous for that?

She laughed with happiness. Whatever happened today, it was for the two of them. She could forget her quest for a while, forget about her father. And hope Luis would forget about his beloved wife.

When Luis and Rachel arrived at the sandy stretch that was south of the town, well away from the influence of the fishing boats, Rachel wondered if she'd misread things. Luis had been as cordial as a good host should be. Yet there had been nothing of what she expected.

Marcos, Luis's driver, drove them. He unloaded a beach umbrella and two folding chairs which he promptly delivered to a wide vacant spot near the water's edge. Rachel marched across the sand, delighted she wouldn't have to lie on a towel, trying to wiggle until she found a comfortable spot. When Marcos returned carrying a cooler, she glanced at Luis. He seemed to think of everything.

The towels Marcos deposited across the back of the chairs were fluffy and large, a colorful rainbow of hues. She would be able to spot their location even if she swam out quite a way.

''Nice,'' she said, sitting on the edge of her chaise and looking around her.

The water lapped at the shore. The pristine white sand reflected the sun so brightly it almost hurt. Glad for her sunglasses, she studied the others on the beach. Mostly families with small children, she watched as they cavorted in the water, ran up and down the beach, or solemnly built castles of sand.

Rachel couldn't remember going to the beach often when she was a child. Her father had been too busy with work, and the succession of housekeepers hadn't wanted to bother.

If she ever married...

She shook her head at the thought. She didn't want to get married. Look at the pitfalls that awaited the unwary.

Sadly, being an only child, she didn't even have the prospect of nieces and nephews to look forward to.

"Not to your liking?" Luis asked.

"What?" She looked at him.

"By your expression, I take it this doesn't suit?"

"Oh, no, I was thinking of something else. This is lovely. With the umbrella I could stay here all day and not worry about burning."

"There's enough reflected rays from the sand and water to take precautions."

She rummaged in her carryall and pulled out a bottle of sunscreen. "Ta da! I came prepared."

Lathering the scented lotion over her legs, Rachel was reminded of afternoons in high school when she and her friends lounged by a pool. With her fair skin she had always needed to take care not to get burned. And she never tanned as darkly as her friend Caroline, try as she might.

"Shall I do your back?" Luis asked.

Rachel froze, her hand stopping on her calf, as she glanced over to him. She did need help where she couldn't reach. But Luis? She swallowed.

"Fine." She could do this. It was only sunscreen.

But the moment his warm fingertips began soothing the lotion over her already heated skin, she wondered if she could hold together. His touch was seductive. The long strokes mesmerizing. His hands felt strong, masculine. She wanted to turn and throw herself into his arms and demand he kiss her as he had before.

Was time moving slowly, or was he taking longer than necessary? It seemed as if the world stood still, only Luis's hands on her back moved. Slowly Rachel let her eyes close. It was heaven.

"Covered," he said, patting her lightly on her shoulder. "Do my back?"

"Sure." She hoped that one word, almost croaked out, sounded normal to him. She did not want to give him any idea of the turmoil that roiled around inside.

His shoulders were wide and muscular. Wearing dress shirts hid his amazing physique. How was he so toned when he worked so many hours in an office, she wondered as her hands traced the defined musculature. His skin was warm, from the sun, or his own internal heat? She poured more lotion on her hand, spreading it evenly, letting her fingertips learn the feel of his skin. She longed to have him turn around.

Almost as if he read her mind, he did. Her hands trailed across his chest. Desire spiraled up inside. Slowly she rubbed the lotion over the chest hair, feeling the rougher texture.

"I can manage," Luis said. His voice sounded low, husky.

Rachel looked up to his eyes, seeing the heat.

"Unless you want me to reciprocate," he suggested, trailing one finger across the top of her bathing suit.

"Uh, no, I already put lotion there." She stumbled back. "I think I'm ready for a swim." She tossed him the bottle and almost ran to the water's edge. Taking a deep breath, she tried to control her wayward thoughts. She hoped the water was cold, she needed something to shock her back to normal.

She plunged in, wading out until it reached the tops of her thighs then dove in. It wasn't cold, but refreshingly cool. She headed for deeper water, swimming for pure joy. She loved the water. And the Mediterranean was especially buoyant. She could swim all day!

"No need to ask if you can swim," Luis said, coming up beside her.

Rachel trod water and shook her hair, water drops flying. "I've been swimming since I was little. But not often at the beach. This is terrific."

"The best part of spending my summers in Spain was the beach."

"Was it hard, splitting your life like that—going first to one parent and then another?"

"Not an ideal childhood. But there were some advantages. If my parents had not separated, I would have spent all my time here and missed out on all I know of America. You spend all of yours in one place, I take it?"

She didn't want to talk about her situation, yet he'd been open with her.

"I lived with my father."

"What happened to your mother?"

She turned and headed back toward land. "If you really want to hear the full story, let's go back."

Dried and enjoying the comfort of the chaise lounge chairs Marcos had brought, Rachel hated to bring up the subject. But she had wondered before if Luis might have some suggestions for searching for her mother. Now was as good a time as any to find out.

"When I was little and asked about my mother, my father always told me she had died. After a while I stopped asking. Then when I was thirteen or so, I asked a lot more questions. Why didn't we have any photos of her? How had she died? Where was she from? You know, the usual things someone would normally learn growing up—almost by osmosis, I guess. I know so little.''

''Did your father answer the questions?''

''Not really. He just said it was so far in the past what did it matter?''

''How did you learn she did not die?''

''Serendipity, I think. Marcella, who is our housekeeper, and I were clearing out some of the stuff in a storage room. There were several boxes of old papers of my father's. We looked through them to see what they were, so we could ask him later if we could toss. In one was a folder concerning my parents' divorce. She didn't die, he divorced her and apparently sent her away.''

''Why did he say she died?''

''To cut me off from her, I guess. I asked him.''

''Ah, confrontation.''

''It wasn't easy, but I was so upset I demanded he tell me about her.'' Rachel remembered the scene. Her father so impervious to her rampant curiosity. Unaware of the blow he'd delivered. So cold!

"And?"

"And I still don't know much more than I did when I found the divorce decree. But I do know now that my father lied to me for more than twenty years. And robbed me of the chance to know my mother."

Luis was silent for a moment. "So you ran away?"

She glared at him. "No, I did not run away. I left. Different thing."

He frowned. "I'm not sure I see the difference."

"I left to regroup. To decide what I want to do. I'm not going to live meekly beneath my father's thumb for the rest of my life."

"And your mother? Have you tried to contact her? Maybe find out why she didn't contact you in over twenty years?"

Rachel took a deep breath. "That's the one fact I can't get by. Why didn't she contact me at some point? If not when I was little, then when I was a teenager? Or when I turned twenty-one.'' She sighed softly and looked at him. ''Or did she just not care enough?''

''That is something you should ask her.''

''I don't know where she is. She could have died in the meantime for all I know.''

''Not likely. She'd be what, in her forties now?''

''I guess.''

''Your father gave no explanation?''

''No. He simply said it was his business, not mine. And so long ago what did it matter? I couldn't get anything out of him.'' Not even a reaction when she said she was leaving. Did he not care for her, either? Had he been stuck with raising her for some reason and was just as happy to have her off his hands one way or the other?

He certainly had been pushing for her engagement to Paul. Marriage would ensure she was taken care of and he'd be totally free for the first time in more than twenty-seven years.

Rachel's mood took a nosedive. Thinking about her life wasn't really awe-inspiring at the moment. But she wasn't going to wallow in self-pity.

"So what are you going to do?"

She raised her chin. "I'm going to find my mother and ask her what happened," she said firmly. "Can you help?"

"Me?" Luis looked surprised. "What can I do?"

"Give me some pointers. I'm sure you know how to find a person who wants to hide. Didn't one of your characters search out someone in book two or three? You must have had to research how to do that."

"Do you think your mother wanted to hide?"

"No. So it should be even easier to find her, don't you think? I've done an Internet search, but came up with nothing."

"She's probably remarried and has a new last name," he said.

She nodded. And a new family which she probably adored. How would she feel to have her long-gone daughter show up out of the blue?

"I did think about hiring a private detective, but thought I should find out all I could by myself first,'' she said. ''Will you really help?''

''I think it could be arranged.''

''For a price.''

''What?''

''Isn't that how the phrase goes—it can be arranged for a price.''

''Cynical?''

''Realistic. What's your price?''

Luis felt a surge of triumph. She was asking what he wanted in exchange for helping her research her mother's location. Should he tell her a night in his bed?

Rachel was a curious mixture of sophistication and innocence. Her confusion when he'd suggested they have an affair was endearing. She was not hardened as Rosalie was. Nor did he any longer believe she was here on some surreptitious newspaper assignment.

She wasn't immune to his touch, or kisses. She'd been responsive as anyone he'd ever held. Which only whetted his appetite for even more.

But finesse would win the day.

"Continue as we've been doing," he said. "When I have a social engagement, you can be my very dear friend from America."

She frowned. He was surprised to find he waited impatiently for her response. He wanted an affirmative.

"Just that, pretend to be friends?"

"What else?" He shrugged.

"What about..." She hesitated a moment and Luis knew what she was thinking about. But he was not making this easy.

"I thought you wanted something more," she said in a rush.

"Ah, our affair?"

She nodded slowly, warily watching him. Did she think he would pounce on her at a beach full of families? The idea irritated him. Didn't she know him better than that? Surely she had some instincts that came into play, even if he hadn't told her his life's story.

"After fiesta, I suspect the entire village thinks we are having an affair, so it changes nothing. We pretend, or we don't. End result is the same." Not quite. He wanted her in his bed, not hers. Vast difference.

"Groupie buster."

"What?"

"You said you wanted me to pretend to be involved to keep groupies away. Groupie buster."

"So Miss Groupie Buster, we still have a deal?"

"We do."

He extended his hand, not to seal the deal so much as to touch her again. Her skin had been like the softest silk when he'd spread the lotion on her back. Her hands had wreaked havoc with his control when she spread the sunscreen on his back. And when he'd turned and she had touched his chest, it was all he'd been able to do to keep from sweeping her into an embrace that would have shocked the families frolicking nearby.

Her handshake was firm. He didn't release her when she thought he should, but tugged gently. She came forward easily, until he could lower his head slightly and brush her lips with his.

It wasn't enough, but would do for now.

Luis settled back, released her hand and tried to look as at ease as he could. "Tell me how you came to be in Spain."

As she spoke he closed his eyes, enjoying listening to her. What had her father been thinking not to tell her the truth long ago? It might not have mattered as much to a young child, but he heard the undertones of hurt in her voice. Discovering the situation at this age had to be shattering.

He'd been sincere when he said he'd try to help. And an affair wasn't the price. He was determined to get her into his bed, but not as payment for his help. He wanted her as involved as he.

As the day progressed, Luis found himself enjoying every aspect. The picnic lunch Esperenza had prepared was delicious. The wine fruity and refreshing. Rachel had been bemused by the spread, declaring the picnics she usually went on weren't so elaborate.

He'd felt a twinge of jealousy when she talked of other picnics, wondering who had shared them with her. Not that it mattered. But for some reason, he wanted today's picnic to remain in her mind for a long time.

Having relieved herself of the burden of her past, Rachel seemed to throw herself wholeheartedly into the day. They swam, lay in the sun for a short time, returning to the shade of the umbrella. Talk was desultory. He learned more about her and knew he was sharing a portion of himself beyond what he normally did with relative strangers.

But while he talked of the past, he never mentioned Bonita, and neither did Rachel.

Marcos returned at four to pick them up. When they reached the *castillo*, Esperenza met them at the door.

"Sophia and Julian will be coming to dinner," she said.

"She invited herself?" he asked, annoyed. "Because I wouldn't commit to going to her place."

"This is still her family home, isn't it?" Esperenza said with a sniff.

"Indeed. I hope it won't inconvenience you to prepare extra for our guests." His sister obviously couldn't wait until he responded to her numerous invitations to dinner. Sophia never had any patience.

When the housekeeper left, Luis stopped Rachel before she reached the stairs.

"We continue what we started at fiesta,"

"For your sister?"

"She is friends with Rosalie."

"But she's your sister. Surely she would side with you."

"If she thinks her actions are for my best interest, she will do whatever she wants." Luis looked forward to playing the enamored suitor for his sister. Let her attend to her own problems and leave him to deal with his as he saw fit.

Rachel wasn't sure she had anything suitable for dinner with Luis's sister and brother-in-law. She showered and then donned a pale pink top matched with one of the skirts she'd brought. Not fancy by any means, but a step up from shorts. She liked the color she'd gotten at the beach, a slight glow always enhanced anyone's looks.

Satisfied she looked the best she was going to given what she had to wear, she descended to the main floor.

Hearing voices, she headed for the formal room near the front door. Sophia and Julian were talking with Luis. She paused a moment in the doorway before they saw her.

Luis had chosen cream pants and a white blouse, opened at the throat. She was surprised to see him in anything other than the black he favored. He looked like casual elegance personified. She wished for a moment it would be just the two of them for dinner. They could continue the pleasant time they'd had at the beach. And who knew, he might kiss her again.

''Ah, Rachel,'' he said, spotting her at the door.

''Hello Sophia, Julian.'' She greeted the guests and took the small aperitif Luis handed her. Taking a sip she was pleased with the tangy taste.

He led her to the sofa and sat beside her. Too close, she thought, feeling his thigh press against hers. For a moment she lost the thread of the conversation, conscious of the awareness that exploded at his touch.

"I'm sorry, what did you ask?" she said, looking at Sophia, doing her best to ignore Luis. He made it even more difficult by laying his arm across the back of the sofa and toying with her hair.

"How long have you known Luis? Where did you meet? I'm so curious. Mama is, too."

Rachel felt Luis start beside her.

"You've talked to Mother about Rachel?" he asked.

"Of course. She's thrilled you are moving on. It's been three years, Luis. We all loved Bonita, but she's gone. She would not have wanted you to mourn her forever."

"She would not have wanted him to mourn her at all. She didn't expect to die so young," Julian murmured.

"Rachel is a guest in my home. Let's not talk of the past."

"So how did you two meet?" Sophia asked again.

Rachel looked at Luis. He was the storyteller in the group, let him answer the question.

His eyes grew amused. Had he read her mind?

"Rachel is an avid fan of my novels. She approached me."

"When you were in America?" Sophia frowned. "You haven't been to the States in three years."

"Ever hear of mail, sister dear?"

"I thought you didn't answer fan mail."

"Where did you get that idea?"

Sophia shrugged, studying the couple on the sofa. "So you invited her here to visit and she came."

"I was in Spain and thought I'd, um, drop by," Rachel said. "Meeting him in person was all I could have hoped for," she said, smiling sweetly at Luis.

He nipped her on her neck, beneath her hair. "As for me, once I saw her, I knew I wanted her."

Rachel's gaze locked with his. He had told her the same thing, but in private. Now he was proclaiming his desire to the world. Her heart fluttered. No one had ever claimed such a thing before. She looked away, meeting Sophia's knowing eyes.

"Here's to getting to know you better," she said, raising her glass slightly.

Rachel nodded, feeling a total fraud. Sophia was a nice woman, she didn't deserve to be deceived by her brother. How was what they were doing any different from what her father had done all her life?

It wasn't quite the same thing, but deceit was deceit. Rachel looked at Sophia.

"It's not quite that way."

Luis put his glass down and reached for Rachel's hand, standing and pulling her up beside him. "Let's go to the patio, Esperenza has set the table there for dinner."

Sophia and Julian rose and led the way.

Luis held Rachel back until they were along.

"What were you about to say?"

"We should tell them the truth. I told you about my father, how he lied to me all my life. I don't want to be doing that to your sister. She deserves the truth."

‘‘This is not the same thing as with your father. We are only leading her to believe something that cannot hurt her in any way.’’

‘‘It’s not right.’’

‘‘Only if it is totally false. We can make sure we don’t lead her astray.’’

‘‘By having an affair?’’

He smiled. Rachel didn’t trust him, but that smile almost melted her bones.

Luis leaned over to kiss her and she was lost. Maybe a small white lie wouldn’t hurt Sophia. And if Luis had his way, they would have a full-blown affair to make everything aboveboard.

‘‘Hurry up, you two, I’m hungry.’’ Sophia’s voice sounded amused more than impatient.

When Luis and Rachel joined the other couple on the patio, Rachel knew her face was pink with embarrassment.

Despite the rocky start, the evening turned out to be more fun than Rachel expected. Once Sophia stopped questioning her about Luis, the conversation turned to Luis’s secondary career as a writer, then to Sophia’s adoration of her baby son, Mario. Julian did not speak much, nor did Rachel.

They enjoyed the meal Esperenza prepared, had coffee with dessert and moved to more comfortable chairs placed on the terrace overlooking the village, which seemed to spread like a sparkling colorful tapestry before them. In the distance a faint glow lit the sky from the lights of Benidorm. The soft night air was redolent with the sweet fragrances of the nearby blossoms.

It was as idyllic a setting as Rachel had ever experienced. For a moment she wished their charade could be true. That she and Luis were falling in love. That it was possible that one day she'd actually live in a castle in Spain.

But reality crashed down. She was not here to fall in love with her temporary employer. In fact, if he would help as he'd suggested at the beach, she might be on her way home before long. Knowing where to find her mother. But still wondering what to do about her father.

Not until she finished transcribing the manuscript, though. She wanted to find out how he wrapped everything up and exposed the killer at the end. She would never again get the chance to type Luis's books and see how he developed the storyline, weaving in clues and red herrings.

One thing at a time. First she had to get through the evening.

Rachel truly felt like one half of a couple by the time Sophia and Julian left. Luis had held her hand while they all conversed easily. He'd been attentive in many ways, making her feel cherished and desired. His touch, a look, a comment made it sound as if they were already intimate friends. The whole thing had her on edge all evening.

Watching Sophia and Julian, Rachel wished she'd found her perfect match. She would love to have the easy, loving relationship they seemed to enjoy. Wistfully she wondered if she'd ever find love.

Shutting the door firmly behind his sister and brother-in-law some time later, Luis turned to Rachel. "Thank you for this evening. It went a long way to convincing Sophia I do not need the services of a matchmaker."

She smiled. "I can't see you needing one even if we didn't pretend that we were more involved than we are."

"Ah, but maybe we are only anticipating things."

"Or not." She stepped away, afraid to become overwhelmed with her own needs to stay close to him. "Good night, Luis." Almost running for her room, Rachel wanted to gain some time alone to regroup. It seemed to become a pattern for her. When overwhelmed, run away. Wasn't that what Luis had suggested, that she was running away?

No more. In the morning, she'd face him. And try to come up with a final answer. She ought to say no. She was already attracted to him. Could easily imagine his ardent words were true, and if she fell in love, where would she be. In a pickle for sure.

Best to say no.

Are you sure? A voice in her mind whispered. She knew the situation going into it. She could guard her heart. And think of the fabulous times she'd have with such a romantic figure of a man. She sighed, once again unsure what she wanted to do. For someone who had always thought herself focused and confident, she was doing a lot of vacillating. Just say yes or no.

The next morning when Rachel went down to the kitchen, Esperenza was not there. A cold breakfast had been left on a tray. A small note told her Esperenza had gone to church, and Luis was out in the olive grove.

Taking the tray, Rachel walked to the stone wall. The panorama was as awesome as always and she sat on the top, balancing her tray beside her. In the distance, she saw two men on horseback, riding up and down the rows of olive trees. She recognized one as Luis and settled back to watch him. Once again he wore black.

He and the dark horse seemed as one. The man with him might be Pablo whom she'd met at fiesta. She wasn't sure. Not wasting time on trying to figure it out, she let herself feast on Luis. She could almost see the play of muscles beneath his loose shirt. Imagine the heat in the sun wearing dark colors. What were they looking for as they rode up and down the endless rows of trees?

A man of many talents and accomplishments. Why would such a man pretend an interest in a stranger like her?

The only answer would be because she was safe, of course. Once she finished the book, or Maria returned, she'd be gone. No long-term commitment. No strings. No need to forget Bonita. An affair would imply to the world he had moved on. And if it didn't work out, there would be others. The well-meant urging of friends would end. He could live life on his own terms, as he was used to doing.

It was Sunday, a day of rest, but Rachel was restless. She wanted to do something beside think, so when she finished eating, and Luis had moved beyond where she could easily watch him, she headed for the study. She'd work on the book to while away the time. Her days were limited and the writing was so compelling she was anxious to find out what happened next.

CHAPTER SEVEN

LUIS RETURNED TO THE HOME sometime later, moving from room to room until he found Rachel in the study, diligently typing. He almost swept into the room and picked her up to carry her upstairs. He didn't remember feeling this sudden spurt of desire with anyone else. Not even his sultry and tempting wife. There was something about Rachel that called to him on a primordial level. She had to feel it. He couldn't be in this alone.

"Have you eaten?" he asked from the doorway. He needed to shower, change. But he needed to see her even more.

She looked up in surprise, a smile breaking out. His heart caught with the sight. She was beautiful.

"Not since earlier. What were you doing in the olive grove?"

"Checking on things. There's a *restaurante* on the edge of town which makes fantastic lamb. Join me?"

"I'd love to. Do I need to change?" She rose and indicated her shorts.

He looked at her legs, then away before he did something foolish. They were lightly tanned, and shapely. He had touched her intimately yesterday, spreading on the sunscreen and when they brushed in the water yesterday. Remembering did nothing for his equilibrium.

"You might wish to wear a skirt. I'd like to leave soon to get there ahead of the after-church crowd. I won't take long to shower."

"I'll be ready," she promised.

He took the stairs two at a time, wishing he'd invited her to join him in the shower—if only to see the shock that he was certain would be her reaction. Rachel seemed too innocent for words sometimes. Was it a ploy? Or was she genuine?

Antonio's was crowded, though there were still two or three tables vacant when they arrived. It was one of Luis's favorite places.

Bonita hadn't liked it particularly. Did that influence his feelings?

Touching Rachel lightly on the back, he guided her toward a table near the edge of the shaded area. The arbor was draped in thick grape vines, their wide leaves sheltering the small green fruit. When the grapes were ripe, customers could reach up and pull down a cluster to enjoy with their meal.

The boisterous camaraderie among the people already enjoying lunch was familiar. He knew most of the people if only by sight. Nodding in greeting, he didn't stop to talk. He was here to be with Rachel, not to mingle.

Soon after they sat at the table, a waiter came over to place their wine down and arrange utensils. He smiled and walked away.

"No menu?" Rachel asked.

"Sunday is lamb."

"That's all?"

"Do you not like it?"

"I do, it's just odd that a *restaurante* this large only serves one dish."

"On Tuesdays, it's fish. Wednesdays is paella."

She laughed. "So you know which day serves what and come accordingly?"

He nodded, watching her as she looked around, taking in everything. No playacting, he'd swear it. She was enchanted with Antonio's.

She looked at him and tilted her head slightly. "So, tell me what you were doing riding all over hill and dale. Checking the olives for what?"

"It is almost time to harvest. Pablo and I were combining a morning ride with checking on the readiness."

"They're still green."

"We don't harvest for table olives, but the oil."

"You explained that before, but I guess I still thought they had to be black and ripe to make oil. After harvest, do you have another fiesta?"

He shook his head. "No. Our fiestas are usually devoted to saints. In years past we had a celebration after the harvest, but not recently."

"Since Bonita's death?" Rachel asked.

He inclined his head once.

Rachel thought it was a shame the people who worked at harvest were denied their celebration because of Luis's wife's death. Maybe one day he would reinstate the tradition.

But she wasn't here to think about his dead wife. He'd invited her to lunch, and she wanted to enjoy every moment. The patio dining was delightful. She loved the grapes growing right above her head, and the view of the sylvan countryside. Spain met every expectation, and then some.

She commented on the setting and soon they were discussing the different regions of Spain—the ones she'd seen and the ones yet to explore. It was heady to have a man focus his intensity on her. She knew she was flirting, but she couldn't help herself. When had she ever had anyone interested in her for herself, not for her father's wealth?

In this case, she knew Luis only wanted a short-term affair. It didn't matter. To have his undivided attention was amazing.

And thrilling.

And sexy.

If he asked her right this moment, she'd say yes.

Lunch was delicious. The lamb so tender she could easily cut it with a fork. The vegetables had been steamed to perfection. The flan afterward melted in her mouth. Feeling replete and a bit sleepy from the fruity wine they'd shared, Rachel wanted nothing more than to relax the rest of her life with Luis.

"Ready to leave?" he asked.

"I hate to go. This has been such a lovely time," she replied with a smile. "Thank you."

"It was my pleasure."

Rachel believed him. He wasn't just saying the words, he'd enjoyed the lunch as much as she had.

Settling back in the convertible a short time later, she was glad he'd driven and not had Marcos chauffeur them. This way she had Luis all to herself. Fantasies began to play in her mind. What if instead of an affair, he asked her to stay? Could she compete with the dead Bonita? Would he tire of her quickly and move on to another?

Not if his devotion to his wife continued. Would anyone ever replace her in his heart?

"Shall we get started on searching for your mother?" he asked when they reached the house.

Rachel felt disappointed. She wasn't sure what she expected after lunch, but searching for her mother wasn't it. She didn't know what she would do with the information if she did locate her. Show up one day and knock on the door? Write? Call?

"That would be fine," she said. At least she'd still spend the rest of the afternoon with Luis.

In only a short time he had the computer hooked up and dialed the access line to get them onto the World Wide Web. Rising, he indicated the chair.

"You need to do this, so you'll remember how."

For the next several minutes, they listed everything Rachel knew about her mother. Then Luis gave her some Web site to try. Nothing turned up.

"Try this one," he said, leaning over and reaching around her to type the address in.

His cheek was scant inches from hers. If she turned her face she could touch him with her lips. Heat enveloped her as she tried to garner enough courage to do just that. One kiss, what could it hurt?

He turned slightly to look at her. "You are not paying attention."

His breath fanned across her cheeks. His dark eyes were all she could see. Almost without volition, she leaned forward and kissed him.

She felt his surprise give way immediately to desire. His mouth moved against hers, opening her lips and teasing her. She replied, feeling on fire. It was the most erotic kiss she'd ever had and only their mouths touched. Their tongues danced, brushed, moved against one another. Yearnings and desire built as the kiss continued.

When he pulled back and gazed into her eyes, she knew he'd see what she was feeling.

"Rachel?"

"Yes," she said.

"Yes?"

She nodded, afraid to break the spell. It might be a reckless move, but it was for her alone to decide. And for once she wanted to feel the passion a man would bring to someone he truly wanted. To experience all the joy of love. To know she was wanted for herself alone.

He cupped her neck gently, tilting her head for another kiss before he stepped back and offered his hand. She rose, placed her hand in his and they walked toward the stairs.

Her heart pounded like a jackhammer, yet she wasn't sure she felt the floor beneath her. She looked at him, dark and dangerous as ever, but so dear to her heart.

No, no, no, she silently admonished herself. *Don't go falling for this man. He would crush your hopes in an instant. This in only for the present.*

But a small part of her acknowledged the futility of her denial. She was already halfway in love with Luis Alvares and going to bed with him was probably the worst thing she could do. And the best thing.

He pushed open the door and led her into the large bedroom. Stopping to kiss her again, he slowly pushed the door closed behind her.

Rachel couldn't help being nervous. She'd never done anything like this before. Would he expect more than she could manage? Or was passion and love something that came naturally? She felt as if she'd known him for a long time at some points. Yet he remained an enigma. Someone she could spend the rest of her life getting to know and understand. Sadly that was not going to happen.

He tangled his fingers in her hair and tilted her head back, sipping at her mouth, trailing kisses down her cheeks, along her jaw. When he moved down her throat, Rachel wondered if her knees would continue to hold her. She gripped his wrists, feeling the pounding of his own blood. It sent her heart rate skyrocketing.

Softly she moaned in delighted pleasure. His mouth returned to hers and she gave herself up to the kiss.

The sunshine streamed in through the tall windows, blazing a path of light across the wide bed. The ornately carved headboard reflected the heavy Spanish style. The dark coverlet emphasized the masculine decor of the room.

Luis moved them closer to the bed, never breaking the kiss. When his hand slipped beneath the cotton top she wore and touched her heated skin, Rachel caught her breath. His fingers touched her like she was precious, skimming lightly against her.

She opened her eyes and leaned back a bit, wishing to savor these new sensations. Her eyes half closed as she let her gaze drift—to come to rest on a large portrait of Bonita Alvares sitting on the dresser, angled to be seen from the bed.

It was as if someone had doused her with cold water. She pulled away.

''I can't do this,'' she said, resettling her top, taking another step. She couldn't stop staring at the picture of Luis's wife. He could see it first thing every morning, last thing every night. This was their room. The room the two of them had shared throughout their marriage. Oh, she was going to be sick.

"What?" Luis looked at her, noticed she was staring and looked behind him. Quickly he moved to the dresser and slammed the photo facedown. "It's not what you think."

"What I think is this is your room, yours and Bonita's. I don't want to be here." She moved to the door, but he was quicker. His hand held it shut.

"Let me out," she said, refusing to look at him. She'd almost made a total idiot of herself. All for a man who still loved his dead wife. How totally *stupid* her fantasies had been.

"Not until you hear me out."

"I don't care to hear anything you have to say."

"I keep her picture there to remind me."

"Oh, well, duh. Why else would someone keep a photo of a loved one?"

"Not for love."

That caught her attention. She risked a quick glance in his direction. He was closer than she'd realized. His gaze was steady. With a sigh, he moved away from the door, rubbing the back of his neck with the hand that had held the door shut.

She turned and leaned against the wooden panels. "What do you mean, not for love? Not for love of who—Bonita? Everyone says you two had the most perfect marriage. The tragedy of her death was more than you could deal with."

"Yeah, well, everyone is wrong. The tragedy is a bloody farce. She was on her way to her lover that night."

Rachel opened her mouth, then promptly shut it. She was dumbfounded. Bonita of the famous loving couple was on her way to a *lover?*

"Unbelievable," she said slowly. "Who could top you?"

He spun around, his expression sardonic. "Is that a compliment? You find it unbelievable she could want someone else?"

"Yes, I do," she said. "Are you saying your beloved wife cheated on you?"

"The proof was in her womb."

Rachel stared at him. "The baby wasn't yours?" she whispered. "Everyone thought—The newspapers said—" She couldn't formulate a coherent thought.

"Yeah, everyone thought the baby was mine. It wasn't and it would have been clearly obvious to anyone who had taken time to find out how far along she was. I'd been in America for three months. Two weeks after I returned home she was dead. Less than six weeks pregnant, I might add."

"That's what you fought about."

He nodded. "I was throwing her out. Divorce isn't something easily obtained in Spain, but separation is. My own parents were separated from shortly after my sister was born until my father died eight years ago. I might have had to stay married to Bonita, but I wasn't going to live with her anymore."

"Everyone thought you two were so happy." Rachel was stunned with the revelation.

"No one knows what goes on in the privacy of people's homes. As long as we jetted here and there, partied long into the night, bought her jewels and fabulous designer clothes, Bonita was happy. Which made our union easier to take. But I was growing tired of all the vapidity we dealt with. I wanted to start a family, settle down. I have enough of a burden running the olive business, and trying to write. I didn't need the rest."

"But she did?"

He shrugged. "So she said."

Rachel couldn't imagine wanting to go elsewhere to meet with strangers and drink away the night when she could stay with Luis—on the patio, or at the gazebo, or their special place on the stone wall.

What a joke, their special place. She was getting in over her head.

"Why didn't you tell anyone?"

"To what end? Her parents live nearby, why hurt them? She was dead, it was enough."

For an instant she remembered the tabloid article suggesting Luis had something to do with his wife's death. If the writer had known the full truth, he would have had a field day with his theory. For that, she was glad Luis had kept quiet.

"I don't understand, why shut yourself away from everyone? Your sister thinks you are still in mourning, Esperenza does. Everyone does, I guess."

"I didn't shut myself away. I continue to run the business, write. What I no longer do is go to parties or fiestas."

"What would it hurt?"

"I don't know her lover's name."

She frowned. "What does that have to do with it?"

"It was someone from the village. That I do know. But who? I have ideas, but nothing concrete. Do you think the man would come and tell me? So when I go there, I look and I wonder—are you the one? Is it a friend who betrayed me? Or an enemy? Or a stranger?"

"Does it matter now, Luis? It's been three years. I know it must have been a horrible shock. But Bonita is dead. The man has to live with the guilt. You have nothing to hide from."

"I'm not hiding. I have no reason to go to those kinds of events. Don't forget, my sister is always hoping to fix me up with another woman. As if I'd ever trust anyone again."

"Wait a minute. Just because Bonita cheated on you, doesn't mean the next woman you get involved with would ever do such a thing.''

''Since you are the next woman I'm becoming involved with, does that mean you?'' The skepticism in his gaze was more than Rachel could stand.

''Yes, dammit, it does. If we have some kind of affair, I'd never look at another man.''

''I'm not talking about an affair. They are quickly over. But what if it were marriage? How long could you or any woman stay loyal? A year, two? My mother lasted seven. Bonita three.''

His mother had left his father. His wife had left him—in a sense. His experience hadn't been all that positive, but that was not the way of every woman in the world. It didn't look as if she was going to convince Luis of that any time soon.

Her bright dreams shattered as she realized he would never look beyond a brief affair with her or any other woman. She'd never admitted to the hope that something wonderful would come of being with him, but it had been there.

She looked around the room, memorizing every piece of furniture, every painting on the wall, the change on the dresser. Even the picture he kept nearby to remind him of his wife's betrayal. This was Luis's bedroom, his most intimate place.

It was probably the only time she'd ever see it.

Rachel fumbled for the doorknob and when found, she turned it. Pulling the door open, she turned and left.

"Rachel."

She had to ignore his call. There was nothing for her with a man who would never trust.

CHAPTER EIGHT

RACHEL FLED TO HER ROOM and closed the door. She wished there was a lock. Surely Luis wouldn't follow her.

Lunch would have to be enough to tide her over until morning. She didn't want to run any risk of seeing Luis again until she had better control over her emotions.

His cynicism dashed any hopes she had of a continuing relationship with him.

His desire for an affair was merely sexual in nature. He didn't want to get to know the real her. He didn't look for anything beyond the next couple of weeks until Maria returned. Any seductive talk had been made with one goal in mind—get her into his bed. And she'd almost gone.

She paced. Anger and unhappiness warring for top spot in her emotions. What she should do is pack her bags and head out. She could find—

What, another job? There were still only 470 Euros in her bag. Less since she'd bought Internet time and breakfast at the café in Benidorm.

Still, it would be better than living in the same house with Luis.

She remembered every kiss, every caress. Closing her eyes against the longing that burned deep inside, she tried to will the images away. But they wouldn't budge. She could almost see them entwined, feel his mouth on her skin, the skim of his fingertips over her most sensitive places.

''Argh!'' She stormed over to the windows and opened them. What she should do and what she was going to do were two different things. She'd done nothing wrong. If he wanted to tie himself up in warped thinking that all women were cheats, that was his misfortune. Once she finished typing the book, she'd get paid and leave.

In the meantime, she'd use the resources he'd suggested to see if she could get a line on her mother. Maybe Caroline could help from her end. Her parents knew some of the same people Rachel's father knew. Maybe Caroline could find out what had happened.

But she'd have to wait until tomorrow to contact her friend. She had no intention of leaving her room today!

Early the next morning, Rachel heard Marcos bring the car to the front. She slipped out of bed. It was pointless to remain, she had been awake since dawn. Standing to one side, hoping no one could see her, she watched. Just like a high school girl longing for a glimpse of some boy she had a crush on, Rachel waited to see Luis.

He emerged from the house dressed in a black suit, silver-grey shirt and dark tie. His briefcase was in his left hand. She'd always think of black as his trademark color.

He spoke to Marcos and climbed into the back of the car without once looking anywhere else.

Business as usual for the man, she thought sadly. His wife betrayed him. Maybe even a friend betrayed him. But instead of letting others know it, he went on alone. Was he always alone? Couldn't he even confide in Sophia?

Rachel watched the car as it turned and headed down the long road to the village. Sadness swept through at the thought of Luis spending all his days merely going to work and then escaping in the world of fiction. He should have a family, learn to laugh, to love.

But she wasn't the one to accomplish that miracle. She had her own problems to deal with and falling in love with some cynical Spaniard wasn't in the cards.

She gripped the drapery. No, she had not fallen in love with the man. She was merely concerned, as any good employee would be, when her boss was upset.

Liar, a voice inside chided.

She turned away from the window and went to get dressed. She'd apply herself to the typing and check the Internet sites they'd found. She would not dwell on anything foolish like imagining herself in love with Luis!

Instead of transcribing the book, however, Rachel became caught up in the search for her mother. She tried the addresses Luis had suggested, getting new ideas and leads from some of them. But nothing pointed her to Loretta Goodson. She wished her father would have just talked to her!

She was in the midst of a long note to Caroline, outlining what she wanted her to do and who she thought the best sources of information might be when Sophia breezed into the study.

"*Hola,* Rachel. I have come to have lunch with you. I understand Luis is off to work. What kind of hospitality is that when you are visiting?"

Rachel looked up in surprise. "Hi, Sophia. I, uh, Luis has work to do. I can entertain myself."

Sophia took in the stack of manuscript pages and looked at Rachel. "You're typing his book?" Her tone suggested Rachel had lost her senses.

"Not right now, I'm sending a message to a friend at home." She looked at the pages, remembering the role she was supposed to be playing. "I've been typing some of it here and there to while away the time when he has to work.''

''He's so consumed with business, he believes everyone else should be as well. Come, we'll eat and then go lie on the beach. It's not often I get an afternoon away from the baby. I want to indulge myself.''

''Let me finish this and I'd love to indulge myself as well!''

''Who is your friend?'' Sophia made no bones about looking over Rachel's shoulder at the message.

''Caroline. She and I have been friends forever.'' Her fingers flew on the keyboard and then she pressed the send key. Since typing the manuscript her speed had increased tremendously. Would she be able to find a job as a real secretary when she returned to the States?

''Let's find Esperenza and have her prepare us one of her delicious salads and then we'll go soak up the sun,'' Sophia said. ''I haven't had a day at the beach in a long time.''

From the deep tan that Sophia sported, Rachel was sure Sophia had more time to indulge herself than maybe she realized. Still, an afternoon away from the castle would be a good thing. At least she wouldn't be thinking about Luis, or her mother.

They took Sophia's car to the beach. Rachel missed Marcos's attentiveness to detail. They had to carry their own things, and the umbrella. No lounge chairs today. No cooler with drinks, only two they had in the totes. Back to normal, she thought wryly.

Once settled near the water, Sophia donned her sunglasses, lay back partially in shade from the umbrella and said, "So tell me how you came to fall in love with my brother."

Rachel carefully put on her own sunglasses. "We're just friends," she said, hoping any color that had stolen into her cheeks would be put down to the sun.

"Come on, I'm family. I've seen the way you look at Luis. It's amazing to me he'd fall in love again. Bonita wasn't the easiest woman in the world to live with."

"Oh?"

"She ran Luis ragged. She was so demanding, wanting this and that. Always on the go.

I think Luis actually prefers a quiet life. You fit perfectly. He's lucky he found you."

Rachel stared at the sea. Was that Sophia's way of saying she was quiet and dull?

"Of course, you will have to stand up to him from time to time." Sophia lowered her glasses and looked at Rachel. "You can do that, right?"

"Oh, yes, I've had my fill of overbearing men dictating what I should do in life."

"Ah, so, tell me all about yourself. Censor nothing!"

Rachel laughed and lay back on her towel, relishing the warmth of the sun, the fresh salt scent from the sea. She'd missed Caroline. No one to confide in over the last few weeks. Not that Sophia would replace Caroline, but girl talk would be a welcomed change!

"I first ran away from home when I was twenty-seven," Rachel began.

Sophia sat up and looked at her. "Are you another storyteller like Luis?"

"No, just giving you my autobiography."

"How old are you?"

"Twenty-seven."

''Ah.'' Sophia lay back down, a grin on her face.

''Do tell all.''

Rachel told of discovering her mother was still alive, of her mixed feelings about finding her, and her burning anger at her father for lying to her most of her life. She was careful to mention nothing about Luis. Sophia put her own spin on it.

''So, you needed a bolt hole and immediately thought about Luis. Wow. And now that you are here, you two are more caught up in each other than worrying about your quest to find your mother.''

''Um, right.'' If Sophia wanted to view everything through romantic glasses, Rachel would let her. She'd know the truth soon enough. And while Rachel felt badly deceiving her, she wouldn't betray Luis for anything. Even in such a small way. It was time he knew he could depend on some people!

Sophia discussed locating missing people, offering suggestions and adding her opinion that Caroline was in a prime position to assist.

"Maybe I should fly over to America and see what I can find out."

"I think we'll manage. I'm curious, however, both you and Luis seemed to have spent much longer in the U.S. than here in Spain, yet you both settled here as adults."

"Umm. Luis was older when our parents separated. He was eight or nine. I was just a toddler, so I don't remember much about living at the *castillo* when I was a child—except for summer vacations. Our father was insistent upon that. And we even had tutors if you can believe it, to make sure we didn't forget Spanish. Of course, he also insisted Luis learn the olive business. I think the separation hit him harder than it did me, because he was leaving the home he'd known all his life, and our Papa. We loved our father. I've never understood quite why our mother couldn't have stayed in love with him. But she seems satisfied now with her new husband. They live in France."

"Do you see her from time to time?"

"Oh, yes, she comes to visit two or three times a year and Julian and I have been up there several times. Luis went once."

Sophia fell silent. "He changed a lot after Bonita's death. Not entirely because of grief, I think."

Probably came from being betrayed by the one person he should have been able to count on above all others, Rachel thought. She and Luis were in the same boat. That should have drawn them closer. Only, after yesterday, there was an impenetrable wall between them.

"Anyway, I came one summer for my visit, fell in love with Julian and so here I live. Luis, of course, once he finished college, was called back to assume his role in the family business."

"Did he wish to do other things?"

"Write, I suppose. His books are wildly popular in the States."

"I know," Rachel said.

"Of course, that's how you two met, you said."

"Tell me a favorite memory of Luis. A time when he laughed, before he became so cynical,'' Rachel said in a rush, hoping to avoid any inquisition into her meeting Luis.

''That doesn't bother you?'' Sophia asked.

''What?''

''His cynicism. His hermit tendencies. His less than sterling opinions of women.''

''That's the only way I've ever known him.''

''When he was younger, he loved to tease me. I remember one time when I was about eight, I guess. He was still a teenager. He and Pablo—did you meet Pablo?—they dressed up as sea monsters. They worked on the costumes for a week, scales and fangs and all. I can still see them rising out of the water—and they scared us to death one day when I came to the beach with some friends. They laughed so hard I thought they might drown. He and Pablo were inseparable when we'd come to visit our father.''

She was silent for a moment. ''It's too bad we had to grow up. I do remember all the fun we had as children.'' She rolled on her side and propped her head on her hand. ''I remember their wedding. I was an attendant. My mother didn't like Bonita, but my father thought she was the perfect foil for my brother. I wonder if he pushed because the marriage would anchored Luis to Spain. I think Papa was always afraid we'd settle in America and he'd not see us after we were grown.''

Rachel kept quiet, though she longed to ask a hundred questions. What had Bonita really been like. Gorgeous, she knew from the newspaper photos. Fiery and temperamental. And dishonest.

''She wasn't very nice,'' Sophia said slowly.

''Who?'' But Rachel knew she meant Bonita.

''Luis's wife.'' Sophia hesitated, then spoke, as if very carefully choosing her words. ''There were rumors in the village about her. I never told Luis. But I often wondered if he knew.''

''You should have talked to him about it. He knew,'' Rachel said.

''What?'' Sophia sat up. ''Luis knew about the rumors? He never said a word. I thought he was truly grieving all this time.''

Rachel nodded. ''He wanted to protect her name after her death. Because of her parents.''

''Wow. Oh, wow! This changes everything.'' She gazed at the sea, her thoughts obviously processing this new slant.

Turning to Rachel, she took off her glasses. ''I meant she was seeing someone else on the side. Maybe more than one man.''

Rachel sat up and nodded. ''He knew, but only at the end. How long had it been going on? Do you know who it was?''

''As far as the rumors are concerned, they started almost as soon as the marriage. You know how a village likes to gossip.''

Rachel didn't know firsthand, but she could imagine. ''Someone should have clued him in earlier,'' she said.

''You think?''

''Wouldn't you rather know than remain in the dark? No matter how hard the truth is to deal with, it's better to know it.'' Hearing her words, she knew when she discovered her mother, she would go and meet her. No matter what, she wanted to know the truth.

* * *

Sophia returned to the *castillo* with Rachel to take a quick shower and then change in the room that had been hers as a child. She told Rachel she wanted to see her brother before heading for home.

"He may be late," Rachel said before going up to change herself. And, she hadn't a clue how he felt. Would he want to continue where they'd left off as if nothing had changed? Or would he put as much distance between them as possible? Should she finish working on the book, or leave?

She didn't want to leave.

"Not if you're here," Sophia said.

Rachel only wished it were true.

To her surprise, Luis was waiting for them in the salon when they had dressed. His dark suit seemed so formal after the weekend. It helped keep their distance. Catching her breath at his look, she felt as if he'd reached out and touched her.

Sophia accepted a small sherry. He handed one to Rachel, his fingers brushing against hers as she reached for the glass. Which almost caused her to drop it. Was she the only one to feel the tension rise in the room?

"Luis, why didn't you tell me about Bonita?" Sophia asked straight away.

He turned. "What about her?"

"That she was a cheat and a deceiver. That you knew she was seeing someone else, maybe more than one someone."

"And you know this how?" He looked at Rachel, his angry gaze promising retribution.

"Don't look at Rachel. It was common knowledge in the village. She wasn't exactly discreet. My money was on Carlos Valdiz, but she also seemed to flirt a lot with Pedro Martinez, and Jose Gonzales."

"You knew, yet you never told me?"

She hesitated. "I guess I thought maybe you knew and didn't care as long as she was not blatant about it. Or, if you didn't know, you would have been appalled to learn the truth."

"But you tell me now."

"I told Rachel, she said you already knew."

"The baby was not mine," he said.

"Oh, Luis!" Sophia reached out to hug her older brother tightly. "I'm so sorry," she whispered, tears in her eyes.

Rachel felt her own throat tighten. What she wouldn't give to have a sibling to share her own dilemma with. Someone who would be there for support, if nothing else.

She turned away and walked into the hallway. She was the outsider, let them have some privacy.

Esperenza set the table on the patio. She looked up when Rachel stepped out of the French doors. "Is Sophia staying for dinner?" she asked.

"I don't think so. She just wanted a word with her brother."

Esperenza nodded and returned to her task.

On impulse, Rachel asked her, "Do you know of any place in the village where I might stay?"

The older woman straightened and looked at her in puzzlement. "You are staying here."

"I know, but it's only temporary. When Maria returns, I won't be needed."

‘‘My cousin’s friend has rooms she rents out. It is on the street where the fountain is. If you wish, I will provide you the information.’’

‘‘Thank you,’’ Rachel said.

Luis stepped out onto the patio.

‘‘Sophia will not be joining us for dinner.’’

‘‘The meal is almost ready,’’ Esperenza said as she headed for the house.

Rachel felt as nervous as could be. She took a deep breath, hoping to calm her nerves, but filled her lungs with Luis’s unique scent. It set her heart to beating.

‘‘I would think you would wish to discuss yesterday,’’ he said softly, his eyes on her.

She shrugged. ‘‘What’s there to discuss? Things…changed. I decided I didn’t want the same thing you wanted.’’

‘‘Nothing changed. Especially the feelings I have for you.’’

‘‘Lust. Take a cold shower.’’

‘‘Lust certainly. But more.’’

She rounded on him, hands on her hips. ‘‘Just how much more?’’

‘‘Do you want to hear about Bonita?’’

"Not particularly. Actually I want to eat, and then go to bed."

"Funny, I have the same goal."

"Alone."

"Ah, we diverge there."

"Luis, stop flirting with me!" She felt surrounded by him, his tantalizing voice, his dark good looks, his intensity.

"And if I don't?"

She swallowed. Staring at him, she tried to read the enigmatic man before her. What game was he playing now?

"I still want you, Rachel." He stepped closer, combing his fingers through her hair. Holding her head gently as he tipped it up to his. "I still want you."

His mouth covered hers in a kiss that spiked her heart rate and sent a spiral of pure sensation through every cell in her body. Rachel found it impossible to keep a coherent thought in her mind. She was too focused on the feelings that swept through. And the one constant, *he still wanted her*.

He didn't push. He didn't force. He merely kissed her until every ounce of sense fled.

She pulled away, putting several feet between them. "It doesn't mean anything," she cried, clenching her hands into fists.

"What do you want it to mean?"

"More than just two people getting together. I…I'm starting to fall for you, Luis. Where would that leave us when Maria returns?"

"Don't confuse this with romance. We are two adults who are attracted to each other. If the exotic setting has you seeing things that aren't there, don't blame me."

"I don't. I think I've come to understand your views of relationships very clearly. Which is why I don't want to proceed any further with where this is heading."

He stepped forward. She retreated a step, watching him warily.

"Dammit, Rachel, I'm not going to pounce on you."

"You don't have to. Just being around you drives me crazy."

He stopped and looked at her. For a moment she thought he would smile. But it had to be a trick of the light, for the next instant she saw those eyes narrow as if considering the next plan of attack.

"You can tell your sister the truth, that you hired me to type your book and we were pretending at fiesta," she said desperately.

"And have her think I'm a liar."

"You are. We are. I feel badly about that."

"So let's make it reality and we don't have to tell anyone anything."

She was so tempted. What could it hurt? He was right, they were two free, willing adults. And she'd have the most fabulous memories to take with her when she left. Who would ever have expected her to catch the interest of such a sexy, dynamic man? He didn't even know how wealthy her father was. This was only about her. Her and Luis.

"What if I fall in love with you," she whispered, revealing her worst fear.

"Ah, *querido,* I can make no promises for the future. Can we not see where our paths lead us?" He stepped closer and held out his hand.

Rachel felt her resistance crumble. She didn't have to fear falling in love if he took her to bed. She'd already tumbled.

Admitting that, could she turn her back on spending time with him? On learning all she could for however long they had together? He'd been burned by Bonita's actions. Could he ever have an open mind about women again? Was it hopeless, or was there a possibility he'd come to care for her?

Dare she pass up the opportunity to try?

She laid her hand in his and went willingly into his arms when he pulled her close.

"I will do my best to make sure you do not fall in love with me," he said solemnly.

She smiled sadly and nodded. "It may be too late."

"And maybe I can find new beliefs to replace old ones," he said as he brought his mouth down on hers.

Luis didn't wish to end the kiss yet, but he heard Esperenza in the hallway. Stepping back from Rachel was one of the hardest things he'd done recently. He enjoyed seeing her flustered when she realized Esperenza was almost upon them. She ran her fingers over her hair in an attempt to smooth it. Her lips were damp and rosy from his mouth. The sight sent a shaft of desire straight through him. He hoped he could contain himself until after dinner.

He seated her at the table as Esperenza placed the bowls and platters in the center. She poured the wine, looking around the meal with satisfaction. Without a word to either of them she returned to the house.

"Do you think she knows?" Rachel whispered.

Luis almost laughed. "Most assuredly. She knows everything." He hesitated a moment, for the first time wondering if that were true. Had she known about Bonita—and not told him? It was likely. She had cousins and friends in the village. If Sophia's pronouncement was true, Esperenza had to have heard the rumors. For a moment anger flared. She had known him all her life, had her loyalties been so divided she kept Bonita's secrets?

Rachel reached out and touched his hand. "What's wrong?"

He cocked an eyebrow at her perception. "Nothing."

She snatched back her hand and began to serve her place from the assortment before them. "If you don't wish to talk about whatever is bothering you, fine. But don't tell me nothing when there is something," she said. Her voice was devoid of expression. Moments before she'd revealed her feelings. Now he'd cut her off.

"I wondered if Esperenza knew about Bonita."

"I doubt it," Rachel said, buttering one of the hot, fragrant rolls.

"Why?"

She looked at him. Would he ever tire of seeing those blue eyes focused on him? Ever get enough of touching her silken skin, the softness of her hair? He was getting aroused sitting at the dinner table.

"From the way she talks about you, she's known you all her life. And adores you. If she had known such a secret, I'm sure she would have told you. Her loyalties did not lie with Bonita."

"How could she not, she knows most of the people in the village."

"Who might have been very circumspect in speaking about the mistress of the *castillo* in the presence of any of her staff."

"You think?"

"Good grief, no wonder you don't socialize in the village if you suspect everyone. Ask her if you want to know. And if she didn't know, you can tell her."

"To what end? I've spent the last three years not talking about it."

"Why? To protect Bonita, or yourself?"

Her question stopped him. Had it been to protect Bonita? Or had he been angry and embarrassed his wife had turned to someone else? Had he wanted to hide that fact from the world? Bonita had known the possible consequences of an extramarital affair. She was gone—protecting her name didn't matter.

Protecting his pride had. Had his not mentioning it changed anything? His wife had still betrayed him. He had still been talked about in the village. And he'd shut himself away from normal activities for years.

Until a blonde on the run opened his eyes. Time to stop playing the outraged husband and begin to live again. With Rachel?

She was watching him warily. She did that a lot. Was he so ferocious?

"Pass the meat, *por favor,*" he said.

She handed him the platter and resumed eating. To defuse the tension, he asked her if Sophia had shown her any pictures of Mario.

Rachel laughed softly and nodded. He could listen to her laughter all day long. Or all night. Her eyes sparkled and her face became even more animated when she laughed.

"About a million. Good thing we were going to the beach instead of her house. If she carries that many with her, how many do they have at home?"

"About ten million. I do believe she takes a roll a day."

"Not really!"

"No, but it sometimes seems like it. He's a cute baby, but I don't need to relive his every living moment."

"Doting parents," she said fondly.

He nodded. At least one couple was doing things right.

"Which it sounds as if neither of us had," she said.

"You don't feel your father was a doting parent?"

"No. Attentive when convenient. Absent when work took precedence. And we know my mother wasn't even in the picture. Were your parents?"

"My father was too busy teaching me duty and responsibility, and hoping my mother's flighty nature had not shown up in my personality. My mother was too busy having a good time to want to do more than annoy my father when the mood struck her. They should never have married."

"Why did they, do you ever wonder?"

"She said she fell in love with Spain. He fell in love with her, I think. But she isn't an easy person to live with."

"Do you ever wonder, what if?"

"What if what?"

"Just what if? What if my mother hadn't left? Would I have a brother or sister, or both?

Would my life have been totally different, or similar to what it is? Would I have felt more comfortable in high school with a mother's guidance? Would my father have spent more time with me and any siblings? What if they had not split?''

"Stupid to dwell on the past and things you can't change.''

"Still, it's interesting to speculate. What if your parents had stayed together?''

He had thought about it often as a teenager. He hadn't thought about it in years, accepting the way things were. But what if they had not separated?

"For one thing, had they stayed together, I wouldn't have been educated in America, never have written my books.''

"Ooh, then it's a good thing they didn't. You have given many the gift of entertainment.''

He was growing used to her compliments. Every time she offered one, he wanted to sweep her into his arms and get confirmation she meant it. That she wasn't just trying to build his ego. Though from the way she resisted any advances, he had had to rethink her plans some time ago. He no longer believed she was a reporter, a groupie, or a woman on the make. She was just who she said she was—a young woman suddenly confronted with a situation she needed time and distance to handle.

She would be leaving once Maria returned. She had her life and he had his. The two could never mix. But for as long as she stayed in Spain, he wanted her here, with him.

He refused to think about when she left.

"Now you tell me a what if?" she instructed.

"What if Bonita hadn't cheated?"

"Oh, then you two would be living happily ever after."

"I doubt that. We didn't live very harmoniously together at the best of times." He had never admitted that before, either. What was she, a witch who could get him to speak of things best left unsaid?

"So what if you didn't write books, what would you do?"

"Work."

"What if you had an exciting hobby?"

He thought of a hobby he'd enjoy—taking her to bed regularly.

"Such as?"

"Skydiving?" She laughed. Had he looked stunned?

"It's not an option."

"Okay, one more. What if you could have anything you wanted, or do anything you wanted, what would it be?"

Luis considered the question. What if he could have anything, do anything? Would he leave the responsibilities of the olive groves, turn his back on his duty and write full-time? He already lived in one of the most beautiful places on earth, he had no desire to change that. But the freedom to do exactly as he pleased?

Or would he rather have something he wanted. Something he thought he'd never want again—a family. A wife who genuinely loved him. Children.

He tossed his napkin on the table and rose. "I don't think I like your game. Life is how it is. What ifs won't change it."

''But what ifs can make you think.''

''I think I've had enough.'' He didn't like where his thoughts were going. He'd tried family life. Maybe one day he'd try again, or maybe just leave the entire family enterprise to his nephew, Mario.

''Are you finished eating?'' She still had half a plate left. He looked at his own, it was also half-full.

''I had a big lunch, I'm not hungry.''

''Well, I am. Nothing like sunshine and fresh air to give me an appetite.''

He wanted her to leave the table and come with him. Where? He couldn't hustle her from the table to bed, much as he'd like to. He glanced at his watch. How long would be a suitable interval? How could she eat so slowly?

He sat back down and watched her.

''I'm not the evening's entertainment. Look at something else,'' she muttered.

But she was this evening's entertainment. And the next few nights until she left as well. Maybe he'd take a day or two off from work and show her parts of Spain she hadn't yet seen. Watch her eyes light up with happiness. See his own country through the adoring eyes of a visitor. Spend enough time with her that he found her flaws and weaknesses and could end the enchantment.

CHAPTER NINE

RACHEL PUT DOWN her fork. "I'm finished. Now what?"

"Shall we take a walk?" he suggested.

"Sure." It would put off the moment she was both anticipating and dreading.

Luis switched on the pathway lighting on the way to the hilltop. They walked side by side where they could, his hand brushing hers. Rachel felt a shiver of delight. The breeze was stronger than earlier. Hearing the leaves rustle in the wind gave rise to fanciful imagining on Rachel's part. Were there wild animals hidden in the darkness?

The lights softly illuminated the gazebo at the summit. But once they stepped inside, Luis turned them off.

"The view is better without lights," he said easily. The village sparkled in the night. Out near the horizon flashes of light appeared.

"What's that?" she asked, pointing.

He stepped closer, more so than really needed to see where she was pointing. She caught her breath. His scent mingled with that of the fragrance of the flowers wafting on the breeze.

‘‘Lightning, I think. There’s a storm coming, can’t you feel it?’’

‘‘Is that why the wind is up?’’

‘‘Yes. I expect it will hit here within the hour.’’

‘‘The rain will be good for the olives, right?’’

‘‘For the most part. When they are ready to harvest, we don’t want them wet. That would hasten the decay and alter the makeup of the oil.’’

‘‘Luis?’’

‘‘Si?’’

She turned to face him. It was too dark to see much of anything, but she thought she was looking up where his face would be.

‘‘I’m ready.’’

‘‘For what?’’

‘‘Whatever comes,’’ she said, reaching out to rub her fingers down the sleeve of his shirt. He’d discarded the suit jacket before dinner.

He seemed to have no difficulty finding her in the dark. His arms swept around her and drew her snug against him.

‘‘Something that comes along like this?’’ he murmured and covered her mouth with his.

Exactly like this, she thought before she stopped thinking entirely and gave herself up to the exquisite sensations his kiss evoked.

Rachel felt as if she floated on the night wind. The touch of his hands on her skin, the feel of his muscles beneath the cotton shirt, the wonderful magic of his mouth and tongue all combined to make her lose all track of time and place. She could only feel. There was no past or future, only the present. There were no problems facing either of them at this moment, only the sheer enjoyment of being with some-one special and making it exceptional.

Lost as she was in delight, she was surprised when a loud clap of thunder shook the gazebo. She looked up, clutching Luis’s shoulder.

''That was close.'' She looked out, the wind was still blowing, and she could smell the rain on the air. In only a moment a torrent poured down.

''Guess we won't be going back to the *castillo* in that,'' she murmured, snuggling even closer. There was no problem. She could stay in Luis's arms all night.

''Unless we wish to be soaked, it would be better to remain here. We have shelter. It's not too cool.''

She laughed softly, tracing his jaw. ''I'm so hot, I could explode. It's not too cool at all!''

''Hot, huh?'' He captured her fingertips and kissed each one sweetly.

''Mmm.''

''Maybe we should do something about that?''

''Like dare me to run into the cold rain?''

''No, like remove some layers of clothing which might be contributing to heat buildup.''

Dropping her hands to his shirt front, she toyed with his tie. ''Am I the only one who has too much on?'' she asked whimsically.

"No." He snatched the tie from his neck and tossed it away.

She unbuttoned the first button feeling the heat that radiated from his body. Excitement raced through her at the thought of touching his chest, learning more about the man who had captured her heart.

She leaned closer and kissed the skin revealed beneath the opening.

"Ah, *querido,* that could prove dangerous."

"I'm forewarned," she murmured.

His hands tangled in her hair and pulled her face up to his for another searing kiss. Soon she was frantic with need. Desire threatened to swamp her. She wanted so much more. To touch and be touched. To kiss and be kissed. To love and be loved.

For an instant she almost faltered. Luis had never said a word about love.

"Let me," he said, easing her shirt over her head. In a flash of lightning she glimpsed him as he caressed her shoulder, watching her in the brief moment of illumination. She loved this man. She wanted to share everything with him.

"Luis, is this a mistake? We hardly know each other."

"You know my darkest secrets, what more do you want? I know yours, right?"

She nodded, stepping closer to close the gap. "I love you," she said inside. And for that love, she would risk anything.

The lightning flashed and the thunder roared, but Rachel didn't notice. She was in a world of two, and for them, it was a wondrous place.

The rain was a steady drizzle now. The fury of the storm had passed long ago. The air was cleaner, scented with the sea. Rachel stirred on the chaise mattress and made an effort to remain awake. She had been drifting toward sleep, lying against Luis, totally and wonderfully satiated. There was something intoxicating about making love in the outdoors. Or maybe it was making love with Luis that elated her.

"Cold?" he asked, his hand sweeping down her back, back up to her shoulder, and hugging her a little closer.

“Just a little.”

“We should get to a bed. A mattress from a chaise isn’t precisely commodious.”

“Complaining already?” she teased.

“Wishing for a bed next time.”

She held her breath. Next time. It sounded wonderful. Then she thought of his room. She didn’t wish to go there. He could come to her room. There would be no lingering memories of Bonita there.

She was jealous of a dead woman. At one time Luis had thought he loved her. Rachel wished he loved her instead.

She sat up, some of the joy of the night fading. “I’ll get dressed.”

“No need on my account,” he murmured.

“I have no intension of traipsing down the path in my birthday suit. Who knows who might be up at this time of night.”

“We won’t turn on the lights. I know the path. I can get us safely to the house.”

“You expect us to walk together, in the rain? With nothing on?” She tried to see him but the rain had obscured any light from the stars and the *castillo* was in darkness so no source from there. This didn't sound like the duty-bound man she was coming to know.

"Think of it as taking a shower together."

She blinked. She had never thought that far ahead. Suddenly the absurdity of it hit her and she laughed. "Okay, if you're game, I am, too. Is this what you learned in Iowa?"

"Hey, don't malign my upbringing. Skinny-dipping is part of the summer-in-Iowa ritual."

"Amazing." He was acting totally different. Was this the real man, the one who had hidden the ache of betrayal behind a facade? Was being with her changing things? Her hopes rose. Maybe they could have something special after all.

They laughed and slid along the pathway. She had her clothes bundled in front of her, Luis had slung his over his shoulder, to keep his hands free to help her. The way they roamed over her back convinced her he wouldn't be much help.

Reaching the house, she held her breath.

"I have to tell you," she whispered as they stepped into the study. "If Esperenza sees us like this, I will die instantly."

"She is long asleep. Come." A moment later he uttered an expletive.

"What?"

"Stubbed my toe. Dammit, I haven't done something like this since I was a teenager."

"I've never done anything like this," she said.

In less than five minutes, they were in Rachel's room.

"Never done anything like this, huh?" he said, taking the clothes from her hands and dropping them on the floor. He pulled her against him, molding her along the long length of his body, he kissed her.

Their trip through the rain had cooled their skin, but his kiss soon had her warm as toast. Damp and hungry for each other, they made it to her bed before the last vestiges of rational thought fled. Luis had a way of making the world disappear.

The sunshine flooding in on her face awoke Rachel the next morning. She frowned, turning away from it, and saw the indentation on the pillow next to her. Luis had stayed the night, but some time ago had left. She vaguely remembered a kiss, and a promise. But she'd been half asleep.

Sitting up, she looked at the clock. It was after eleven!

Good heavens, what would Esperenza think?

She showered and dressed in record time. Making her way to the lower floor a short time later, she saw one of the maids vacuuming in the drawing room. Esperenza might be in the kitchen, though it was too early to be preparing lunch and breakfast certainly was long over.

Rachel could do without food for a while. Maybe she could just pretend everything was normal and expect lunch at one like most days.

She sat behind the computer, staring at the stack of paper to be typed. She was more than halfway through. A few diligent days of effort and she might finish before Maria returned.

''There you are. I have a message for you,'' Esperenza said from the doorway.

Rachel smiled, feeling heat flood her cheeks. ''Good morning, what message?''

"Luis said to take the car and meet him at the café by the marina in Calpe. And to wear walking shoes and cool clothes."

"Calpe? Where is that?"

"If you take the road to the village, when you reach main street, turn to the left and follow the coast until you see the signs for Calpe. There is a sidewalk café near the marina. You can drive the car, right?"

Drive Luis's convertible? "Of course." She jumped up, the typing forgotten. "I'll get my shoes and head out. Did he say what time?"

"No, but for lunch. So I would leave soon. Pay attention to your driving. This is not California."

"If I can drive in Los Angeles, I can drive anywhere!" She almost hugged Esperenza in her exuberance. Luis wanted her to meet him for lunch at a seaside café. It sounded like the perfect romantic place. She wasn't sure about the walking shoes, but put on her most comfortable pair.

She shook her head as she drove down the winding road, enjoying the feel of the wind. This car was a dream and she savored every moment. Who would have thought a few weeks ago she would be dashing to meet the man she loved. She thought of her father, and Paul. She'd have to do something before long. Let her father know where she was. She knew he'd be worried about her. He had to realize, however, how things had altered between them.

Not that anything had changed about Paul. But maybe her father would talk to the man and make sure he knew Rachel wouldn't consider marrying him in a million years. Especially after meeting Luis. Not that she planned to share that information with her father just yet.

Traffic was light on the coast road and she enjoyed the drive, darting glances at the Mediterranean Sea as often as she dared. The play of colors from pale turquoise to indigo continued to fascinate her.

She found the place without any difficulty. Hurrying from the car, she saw Luis. He was watching her. Rachel swallowed, hoping she didn't make a total fool of herself. She was so happy she could skip.

He rose when she approached the table.

"Thank you for letting me drive that car," she said breathlessly, stopping beside him.

He brushed his mouth against hers and then held a chair for her. The large umbrellas sheltered the tables from the sun. The road passed between the café and the sea, but except for the occasional car, their view was unimpeded.

She smiled at him. "This is terrific."

"I'm glad you came."

He'd changed from his suit into more casual attire. She looked around, but no one was paying them any attention. Had he chosen this place for privacy?

"So what's up that I needed walking shoes?" she asked once their lunch order had been placed.

"I thought we could climb El Pẽnon de Ifach after lunch." He indicated a mammoth rock formation jutting into the sea. It towered over the town.

"You can climb that?"

"There is a path on the back side. The view from the top is worth the trek."

Walking on the back side of the moon would be worth the trek if Luis were with her, she thought. "Sounds like fun. Shouldn't you be working?"

"I took the afternoon off. Marcos dropped me here. We'll take the car back together."

She looked around.

"Something wrong?"

"I'm looking for Luis Alvares. You look like him, but certainly don't act like him."

His eyes lit in amusement. "I think you have freed me from the shackles of the past."

"Wow, that's the most romantic thing anyone has ever told me," she said, stunned. Did he really mean it?"

He took her hand in his. "Seriously, Rachel, I want to show you some of Spain. You love my country. Let me share my favorite spots with you."

Seriously. He had been joking. But she didn't care. To joke was enough of a change to suspect something more had happened. And to have him show her his special places was more than she ever expected. Who knew, if they were together long enough, maybe he would fall in love with her. Wasn't love contagious?

Treasuring every moment of the afternoon, Rachel knew it would be a special memory for many years. They ate and then headed for El Pẽnon. Luis made sure they had water bottles and sunscreen.

It didn't take long before the pathway steepened and walking became more than a saunter. But every time Rachel paused for breath, she had a better view. They passed tourists on the trail and nodded. When they reached the summit, Luis casually put his arm around her shoulders, drawing her closer as he pointed out places of interest. Their luncheon café looked like a miniature diorama from this viewpoint.

She dutifully looked but was too conscious of his closeness, of his touch, to pay attention. When he paused, she turned her head and looked at him. He was gazing down at her.

"Did last night really happen?" she said.

His kiss blotted out the view, the sun, the memory. A new one was in the making.

When they heard the voices of another couple nearing the summit, they broke apart.

* * *

"Not as private as the *castillo*," Luis said, brushing back her hair from her cheek. The tendrils were as soft as down. He wished he could wrap the tendrils around his fingers and let them drift through. Then he'd like to kiss her again, feeling the passion she displayed last night.

The other couple reached the wide cleared space at the top and exclaimed over the view. Luis wished they had timed their arrival for later—like next week. But he nodded cordially when they called greetings.

"Have you seen enough?" he asked.

Rachel sighed. "I don't think I could ever see enough. This is different from the view at the *castillo*, but both are sensational. I could stay here all my life."

"It gets cold when the wind picks up and there aren't a lot of amenities," he said, resting his hand on her shoulder. She was fine-boned. He longed to slip beneath her shirt and feel the silky texture of her skin. Kiss her again and taste her unique sweetness.

He was growing hot and aroused just thinking about what he wanted to do. Now was not the time nor the place. They still had to return down the steep path and get to the car. And then home. Suddenly Luis was impatient. He had denied himself for far too long because of Bonita.

Was he trying to make up for lost time?

No, he'd had opportunities over the last three years. But no one had appealed to him like Rachel. If he was in a hurry, it was because Maria was returning soon and Rachel would leave. Make hay while the sun shines, had been a favorite saying of his Iowa grandfather.

"But I'll leave if I can come again," she said, leaning against him just a little, in a cozy, companionable way. He liked it. He liked most things about his surprise secretary. He knew he'd miss her when she left.

"You can come again whenever you wish. I'll try to come with you, if you like."

"Definitely!" She smiled up at him and Luis felt his desire spike. She was beautiful when she smiled. Her entire face seemed to light up. Her blue eyes shone with happiness.

Pride puffed up when he knew being with him enhanced that happiness.

They had an easier time going down the path and it didn't take long before they were back at the car.

"Home?" he asked as he closed the passenger door behind her.

"Can we drive along the coast for a little longer? I loved the stretch between here and the village. What's ahead?"

He slid behind the wheel and adjusted the mirrors. "It's the same for the next fifty miles."

In only moments they were flying along. The sea was to their right as they headed north, the sun overhead. Ahead, the road was virtually deserted. He glanced at her and saw her delight. She wasn't a woman to hide her thoughts. Was she too good to be true? He settled in and began to enjoy the drive as well. It had been too many years since he'd traveled this stretch of road for anything but business.

"Thank you for a wonderful afternoon," Rachel said as he pulled in front of the house and stopped. He killed the engine and turned slightly to look at her. ‘‘My pleasure.’’

‘‘Mine, too. I’ll remember today forever!’’

‘‘Tomorrow, join me for dinner in Benidorm?’’ The least little thing seemed to please her. How would dinner and dancing at one of the supper clubs be? He could hold her in his arms and move with the music. And later, hold her in his arms again and move to the music the two of them would make.

‘‘Not dressy?’’ she asked.

‘‘A bit. Come in to town early and shop.’’

‘‘I guess.’’

He could have hoped for a more enthusiastic response, but he’d take what he’d get. ‘‘I’ll have Marcos pick you up after lunch. He can bring us back after dinner.’’

‘‘Is there some reason you asked me now rather than later?’’ she asked.

‘‘No.’’ He just wanted to make sure he had tomorrow lined up.

When it came time to retire for the night, Luis didn’t give Rachel any choice. He went up with her and into her room. When she looked in surprise, he swept her into a kiss before she could say anything. He knew how she responded to his kisses and was using that to make sure he stayed. The ticking clock sounded louder in his mind. She'd be gone soon.

Before drifting to sleep some time later, he gathered her close. "I spoke with Esperenza," he said softly.

"About what?" Rachel's body was warm and soft. He could hold her forever.

"About Bonita. You were right—she never knew. But she does now. Never underestimate the gossip network in a small village. Carlos Valdiz was Bonita's lover."

Rachel sat up and looked at him in the dark. "How did she find out?"

"Once she learned of Bonita's deception, she called her cousins and brother and aunt. In no time they'd found someone who had seen Bonita more than once leaving Carlos's flat late at night. So now I know who."

"And does it help?"

He shrugged, more intent on Rachel than lost loves of the past. "He and I were never friends. I can avoid him in the future and let the past rest. Lie back down, I like feeling you against me."

She snuggled closer, as if trying to ease the pain of discovery. Luis was intrigued to find he really didn't care after all these years. Bonita was in the past. Rachel was his present. And maybe his future?

Rachel sat in the back of the car the next afternoon feeling like a princess. Marcos hadn't responded to her attempts to be friendly, so she assumed he liked silence when he drove. She held her bag, gazing out the window. She'd love to buy the most fabulous dress she could find to knock Luis's eyes out, but she was very conscious of her dwindling Euros. She hoped she could find something suitable which didn't cost the earth. She'd brought her pumps. They weren't the sexy strappy shoes she had at home—in California she corrected herself. But they would go with almost anything and look presentable.

She looked forward to shopping, though wished Caroline was going with her. She could hardly wait to tell Luis her news. Her dear friend had come through for her in spades!

Despite her concerns, Rachel found a dress she thought would be perfect and didn't cost too much. A deep maroon, the little slip dress faithfully followed her curves and valleys. It was the sexiest thing she'd ever worn. She couldn't wait for Luis's reaction.

It was all she could have wished for—he stopped for a moment when he crossed the lobby of the building. She'd slipped out of the car and gone to meet him, hoping for just such a reaction. Much more satisfying than having him slide into the back seat with her and not get the full effect at once.

He continued across the expanse, the heat in his eyes all she could have wished for. Her heart leaped in response.

"You are beautiful," he said softly. When he drew close enough, he kissed her. Right there in the lobby of the building in which his offices were located. Rachel was stunned he claimed her so openly.

''It's a little early for dinner, I thought we could visit one of the bars on the beach and listen to the music for a while.''

''On the beach?'' Her shoes weren't exactly the best for walking in the sand.

''At the beach perhaps is more accurate. We don't have to traipse through the sand.''

Great, now he was starting to read her mind.

He walked beside her to the car, and ushered her into the back seat. Giving Marcos the directions, he settled in, and took one of her hands in his.

''Tell me what you did today?'' he said.

''Typed on your book, of course.''

''That's all? There's an air of excitement here, and I don't think it's from chapter eleven.''

''I'm on chapter fifteen, thank you very much. You must be falling behind on reading the transcription. And I do have news, but I'll wait until we're at the table.''

''Good news, I take it?''

''The best.'' She smiled at him, glad she could share it with him. But she didn't want to be interrupted if they arrived before she finished telling him all the details. It would wait a few more minutes.

The bar was charming. Definitely casual—they were the most overdressed couple there. Parents had brought children ranging from babies to pseudo-bored teenagers. Everyone was enjoying themselves as evidenced from the laughter and boisterous conversations. There were no walls, just supports to hold the roof. Beyond was the wide expanse of beach and the sparkling sea.

They found a table near the edge of the sand. Once their waiter had taken their order for white wine, Rachel leaned forward.

"I found my mother!"

"What?"

She nodded, her heart tripping. "Caroline asked around for me, questioning people who have known my father long enough to remember my mother as well. She ended up speaking with Harvey McMichels—whose mother is an avid genealogist. So Harvey put Caroline in touch with his mother who gave her even more ways to track someone down than you gave me. I found out her high school, went to a Web site for the school and got in contact with someone who knew my mother as a girl. And still keeps in touch! But the best part was Harvey's mother actually remembered the divorce. She told Caroline all about it.''

''What happened?'' Luis asked.

''My father was just as devoted to work in those days as he is now. My mother felt neglected. She began to drink rather heavily. One day she was in a solo car accident, due to being intoxicated. That was all my father needed to get her to agree to a divorce, and to leave me behind. He was worried about my safety.''

''And she agreed?''

''Must have, I haven't heard from her in all these years.''

Luis leaned back in his chair and gazed off at the sea lost in thought for a moment.

''There must have been more for her to stay out of your life all this time,'' he said finally.

''Well I don't know what it was. Maybe he did have good reasons for lying all these years. Maybe she really didn't care about me.''

''Have you contacted the woman who knew her from high school?''

"Yes, I sent an e-mail and she already responded."

"You told her who you were?" he asked.

"No. I just said I was trying to find her. I know where she lives, San Antonio, Texas. She did remarry. I have three half-siblings, two brothers and a sister."

It still seemed surreal to Rachel. One moment she wondered if she'd ever find her mother, or discover what happened between her and her father, and the next, she had it all. Her feeling toward her father had changed slightly. She tried to look at the situation from his point of view twenty years ago. A wife who couldn't be trusted with their child. She still didn't know what had kept her mother quiet all these years, but no matter what, she wanted to know.

Luis lifted her hand to his lips, kissing the palm. "This calls for celebration. We should be drinking champagne, not mere wine."

"Being with you is celebration enough." She was giddy with sensations. His kiss had her wishing they could forgo dinner and return home. Her elation over locating her mother had her high as a kite. And being with Luis was celebration enough for everything.

She wasn't sure what caused the change, but he was definitely as interested in her as she was in him. She cherished every moment, amazed she could interest a man like him. And knowing it was she he was interested in, not her father's daughter. Who would have thought fleeing California would have ended up with more happiness than she could hold?

He questioned every step, congratulating her on her methodology, speculating with her on the best way to approach the woman. He offered some suggestions about finding out more about the situation before flying to Texas where her mother now lived. Rachel was grateful for all the advice. She wished she were brave enough to ask him to accompany her.

Dinner was romantic. She watched him order over the candles that graced their tables. The dinner club was the epitome of elegance. The starchy white tablecloths, the heavy silver, the fine crystal gave a festive air to their meal.

When the dancing began, Rachel knew she was in heaven. Luis was the perfect partner.

She could have danced all night except for the awareness that rose every time she touched him, every instant when they turned in time to the music. Just being with Luis had her hungering for more. Wrapped in a rosy, romantic glow, she enjoyed the evening, but yearned for what she knew would follow. The last two days had been the happiest in her life.

Maybe discovering her father's lie had been fate. Otherwise she would never have met Luis. Or fallen in love.

He looked content to be with her. His gaze never wandered to others on the dance floor. He wasn't looking to see who was around he might also wish to dance with. He was focused solely on her.

Excitement licked in her veins. People were supposed to pair up, and offer love and support all their lives. She didn't know why some marriages didn't turn out that way, but if she married she'd do all in her power to make sure it lasted until death.

Would he ask her to share his life with him? Could she live in Spain? Of course they would make trips to the States. She'd miss Caroline and some of her other friends, but they could come to visit. She wouldn't mind, as long as she had Luis.

"It is late. We should be heading home," he said as a slow song ended.

Still wrapped in his arms, Rachel nodded. She hated to see the evening end, but there would be others.

As Marcos whisked them along the coast road, Luis leaned back. "This weekend, would you like to go to Madrid? I have a small apartment there. We could visit the museum, stroll La Plaza d'Espana, make sure you see as much of the city as we have time for."

"I'd love to." A vague feeling of uncertainty pricked. It sounded if they didn't have forever to explore Spain's capital city. She shook it off. It was just the way he said it. They'd have time again to visit.

"Then I will take off work early on Friday and we'll fly up that evening. That will give us two entire days."

"Sounds wonderful." Of course, picking olives at harvest time sounded wonderful if she could do it with him.

* * *

Rachel spent the days until Friday transcribing manuscript pages and searching the Internet for more information on her mother. She had a home address, a phone number, information about her husband, who was a tax consultant, and the three younger siblings she didn't know she had. Two were in college, one in high school.

She debated calling. But was afraid her mother would hang up on her. What if she hadn't told her new family about Rachel? What if contacting her would result in rejection?

She discussed it with Luis each night. They had had dinner at the terrace, telling Esperenza not to pick up the dishes until the morning. Rachel knew Esperenza must suspect more was going on than dinner, but the older woman never gave a clue as to her feelings about it.

Sophia came for lunch one day and commented on how well Rachel looked.

Of course, she was a woman in love.

Friday Luis arrived home in time for lunch on the patio. As they were finishing, Esperenza arrived in the doorway, an odd look on her face. She looked at Rachel.

"There is someone here to see you."

Rachel rose. "Sophia?"

"No, darling, it's me." Paul Cambrick stepped into the doorway.

CHAPTER TEN

RACHEL SAT DOWN HARD. The last person she had expected to see was Paul. "What are you doing here?" she asked.

Luis rose to face the man. "Who are you?"

"Paul Cambrick." He came forward, his hand extended.

Luis looked down his nose. Rachel admired his aristocratic gesture. Not many people put Paul off. What was he doing here? How had he found her? She looked beyond him. Had her father come as well?

"Are you a friend of Rachel's?" Luis asked, ignoring the extended hand.

"Fiancé, actually."

"No!" Rachel surged to her feet once more, coming around the table. "That's not so."

"Lover's quarrel," Paul said to Luis, man to man. He turned to Rachel as she stormed around the table. "Your father would have come, but I told him I could handle this. Time you got over your snit, sweetheart, and came home.''

''I'm not in a snit. And I'm not your sweetheart!'' She turned to Luis, her heart sinking. She was familiar with that closed-off look.

''Luis, I'm not engaged to him.''

''Rachel, shame on you. Have you been leading this man on? You have my ring. How much more do you need?''

''We'd need to care about one another for one thing. And I care nothing for you.'' The ring had sat on her dresser in her room in California. Paul had urged her to keep it while she thought over her answer, not accepting her refusal all those weeks ago. She'd told her father to give it back to Paul.

Luis withdrew, she could feel him do it, though he didn't move a muscle.

''Perhaps you need time to get your life in order,'' he said to Rachel. ''I should have known better. But do you know, for a while—'' He stopped abruptly and with a slight nod, left them on the patio and entered the house.

Rachel rounded on Paul.

"I don't know how you found me, or why you went to all the trouble of coming here, but in case you aren't getting the picture, I'll make it clear as glass. Get away from me and leave me alone!"

"Your father sent me. I'm here to take you home and we are getting married. Once we are married, I don't expect to have to go chasing halfway around the world for you, either."

"Paul, read my lips, I will never marry you."

Anger flashed in his eyes. "You will. Your father supports the idea. We've already discussed partnerships. How will you manage without someone to support you?" He glanced around the patio, taking in the back side of the *castillo*. "It looks like you are trying for even bigger stakes."

"You're delusional if you think I plan to go home and dutifully marry you. Whatever deal you and my father work out is between the two of you. Do not use me as part of the deal. I told my father to return your ring. Do with it whatever you two wish, but leave me alone!"

''Your father misses you, Rachel. Come home. We'll discuss this later, when you are not so emotional.''

''What part of 'go away' do you not understand?''

She needed to find Luis, to explain. She couldn't forget the shuttered look when Paul told him she was his fiancée. He probably thought she had cheated even as Bonita had. She had to find him. Walking toward the house, she stopped when Paul caught her arm.

''I've gone to a lot of trouble to track you down and find you. Leaving without you is not an option,'' he growled.

''How did you find me?''

His smug smile made her want to knock it off his face. Where was Luis? He couldn't believe she would have led him on while she really had a fiancé in her life. He had to know her better than that!

''Caroline bragged to Marty Henson. Marty was showing off at some tennis party a couple of weeks ago, and telling one and all how her friend Rachel had a job with a famous author. From there, it was just a matter of time.''

She remembered that early e-mail to Caroline. Why hadn't she kept quiet? Or why had Caroline told Marty? Water over the dam now. But that didn't mean she planned to meekly leave with Paul and return to her father's house. She had more important things to do—like find Luis.

"Just go, Paul."

"I'm not going without you," he repeated.

"Then I guess you are planning to live in Spain, because I'm not leaving."

Esperenza came to the door, her face troubled. "Señor Alvares has asked me to help you pack, Señorita." She threw an angry look at Paul.

"There, you see, you can no longer stay here. I've booked us both on a flight from Madrid tomorrow."

She shook off his hand. Head held high, she swept past him and Esperenza. So Luis wanted her to leave, did he? Was he too cowardly to tell her himself? To listen to her explanation?

Esperenza followed Rachel to her room.

"I really need to talk to Luis," she said, turning as she reached her door.

"He left. He will be back later, but asked to make sure you were gone before he returns. I'm sorry," Esperenza said.

Rachel reeled as if she'd been struck. He wouldn't even listen to her? Granted there was a smidgen of a correlation to the experiences he'd had with Bonita, but he needed to hear the truth. How could he ignore her and leave like that? What if she needed—

The truth hit her. He didn't care. These last few days had not been courtship, but the affair he'd originally asked for. To him it just ended earlier. The only difference was in her mind, not his. He'd never promised her anything.

Stunned, she entered the room. She'd pack and leave the *castillo*. But if he or Paul thought she would go meekly back to California, both of them were in for a surprise.

"I'm not leaving until I speak with Luis," she vowed.

"Señorita, he won't be back until you are gone."

"So I'll go to the village. Your cousin's friend still has a room I could use, right?"

''*Si.*'' Esperenza smiled at this. ''*Si,* she'll give you a break in the rate, if I tell her.''

''Thank you.'' Now Rachel just had to figure out how to get rid of Paul. If Luis didn't want her, there was no need to remain. But she was not going meekly back to her father. Not until she'd met her mother. Then she'd make up her mind what she would do in the future.

Packing, she tried to ignore the knot in her chest, the tears that threatened. Folding the maroon slip dress, she remembered their dances. Placing her swimsuit in the case, she remembered their day at the beach, spreading the sunscreen on Luis's back. Memories of El Pẽnon in Calpe, of the fiesta, of Sophia and Julian all crowded in her mind as she looked one more time around the room to make sure she'd forgotten nothing.

She was leaving with all she'd arrived with. Except her heart. That would remain with Luis. Maybe forever.

''Esperenza, do not tell anyone where I've gone,'' Rachel said as she lifted the small case. ''I'll lose Paul when we get to the village and stay out of the way until he gets fed up and leaves.''

She doubted Luis would even ask. Her heart broke a little more when she realized she wouldn't see him again if he had anything to do with it. All she wanted was to feel his arms around her, hear his voice reassuring her. Offering support for her choices.

Taking a deep breath, she tried to smile. So be it. ''Thanks for everything, Esperenza. Maria will have to finish the book. I was so close, too.''

Esperenza led the way to the large foyer where Rachel had first made her pitch for a job.

Paul paced there.

She tilted her head. Time the men in her life knew she wasn't a pawn in their games.

''Let's go, Paul,'' she said. In only a short time, she'd disappear again. Let him find her after that!

Luis climbed to the gazebo and walked to the railing. Here he'd first made love to Rachel. He tightened his grip on the wood and gazed out across the olive grove. He had been played for a fool a second time. Those wide blue eyes had not been guileless. What was her game? Did she enjoy pitting one man against another? Had she grown tired of life in California and was looking for more excitement, more variety? Nothing like being aligned with a famous author to get vicarious fame. He knew that from Bonita.

Rachel wouldn't be here for the harvest. He knew their time together had been limited. Maria would be returning soon. It had only been a summer fling. He never intended for it to go any further.

They'd had some fun. It was over.

So why did it feel as if there was an aching hole in his chest? Why did he wonder where she was? Why torment himself with images of her and Paul in some hotel room?

''Dammit!'' He turned away. The fading light muted the colors of the sea, but he gazed over the water, remembering her delight at the café in Calpe. And her constant wonder at the view from the *castillo*. Would he ever stop thinking about her? Not want her?

He had let her off too easily. Bonita had run when he'd discovered her cheating. He'd sent Rachel away. He should have told her first what he thought of women like her. Told Paul all that had transpired. Would the man still want her for a wife after that?

Thinking about it a moment, it struck Luis there hadn't been much of a loverlike attitude from the man. And Rachel had denied their engagement. Of course, what else would he expect? She certainly wouldn't brazen it out by confessing.

It would be a long time before he let himself get involved with another woman. Twice burnt was lesson enough for any man. It was a long time before he left the gazebo.

Rachel had found it easy to escape Paul. He never expected her to even try it, she was sure. Esperenza's cousin's friend welcomed her into her home and gave her a lovely room which overlooked the small garden. Beyond, rising above the town, the grey *castillo* loomed. Rachel had spent most of the afternoon staring at the castle and wondering what Luis was doing. He had not given her a chance to talk to him. He had sent her away thinking she'd betrayed Paul in the same manner Bonita had betrayed him.

But it wasn't the same at all. And she wanted him to see he was wrong. She was not like his wife!

In the end, did it matter? He had wanted a summer affair. Maybe it would be easier to make the break this way. For him, Paul's arrival had just ended their affair a bit earlier than Luis's schedule.

Tears welled, but she brushed them aside. She wasn't so sad as angry! She would not leave until he'd heard her out. If nothing else, she wanted him to remember her favorably. She refused to leave until she knew he didn't believe she would have cheated on a man as his wife had done. She possessed more honor than that.

In the meanwhile, it was past time to contact her father.

The next morning Rachel braved the local taxi driver again and headed up to the *castillo*.

Ringing the bell, she rehearsed what she would say.

To her dismay, when Esperenza opened the door, she shook her head. "He is gone, Rachel. He left early this morning. He said not to expect him back for some time."

"Oh. I came to explain about Paul." Disappointment filled her. She had counted on making him understand. "You don't have any idea when he might be back?"

Esperenza shook her head, sympathy in her eyes.

"I guess I'll check back in a few days, then."

She turned. Once again she'd sent the driver away. Now what was she going to do?

"I'll need to call for a cab," she said.

"If you can wait a while, I plan to visit a friend this afternoon. I can give you a ride to the village then," Esperenza offered.

"Thanks, I'd appreciate that. It's not as if I have anything else to do. Maybe I could transcribe some more of the manuscript while I wait."

When Esperenza hesitated, Rachel shrugged. "It's no big deal. I've seen most of the book. I'm not rushing somewhere to give it away. But if you are uncomfortable with me in the house—"

"Of course not, Señorita, come." She opened the door wide. "I'll prepare lunch at one and we can leave after that."

"You don't need to feed me."

"Come in and don't argue."

Rachel smiled sadly, wishing she'd gotten to know this kind woman better.

Settled behind the computer moments later, she began to type. Maybe while Luis was away, she could catch up and finish the book.

Maybe he could pay her for the work, too. He'd never discussed compensation the first day. Living in his home had meant she'd had to spend very few of her Euros, but still, he owed her for her time and the pages she'd done.

A thought struck her. Her father now knew where she was. She needn't hide any longer. She could use her credit cards and her bank card!

She stopped for lunch, and then resumed typing while Esperenza cleaned up and got ready to visit her friend. Lost in the book's convoluted plot, knowing she was approaching the end, she hoped she could figure out who the murderer was before Luis revealed it. She jumped when a blue square landed on the desk. It was her passport.

"It's hard to leave the country without it," Luis said.

She looked up, her heart leaping at the sight of him. His demeanor wasn't very approachable, but just to see him warmed her heart. "I forgot you had it."

"You would have remembered if you had tried to get a flight from Madrid. I went to the international counter, but you weren't there."

"You went to Madrid? Just to give me my passport?"

"No, not to give it to you. But to talk you into returning here."

"I wasn't leaving."

"Oh?"

"Paul left, I think."

"You don't know?"

"I ditched him."

"What?"

"Ditched him. Escaped. Left him on his own."

"I know what ditched means. Why?"

"I told you yesterday, I am not nor have ever been engaged to Paul Cambrick. He wishes I were, but not for me. He and my father could make lots of money if they merged operations. Actually, Paul would make more than he has now, and my father always likes opportunities like that, so it would be beneficial to both of them—"

He leaned over and put his fingers over her mouth. "You are talking about a man I don't care if I ever hear about again."

She blinked. The touch of his fingers sent her heart skyrocketing.

"Okay, I won't speak of him again. What shall we talk about? Tell me again why you went to Madrid."

"To bring you back. What you are doing here?"

"Typing your book. I'm almost finished. I have to know before I go who did it. If you don't want me to finish transcribing it, then I need to read to the end really quick.''

''I thought you had left,'' Luis said.

''Well, I hadn't made you understand, so I couldn't leave.''

''Understand what?''

''That I had not acted like Bonita. That I had not cheated on anyone. And that I would never have hurt you or anyone else in such a manner. I must say I was surprised you thought so little of me that you'd believe it even for a moment.'' And hurt. But she need not reveal that tidbit.

''All I could think of was you were just like Bonita. That no woman could be trusted.''

''That much was obvious.''

''Then I began to remember the time we spent together. How outraged you were when you learned about Bonita. The determination you showed in defying your father and his wishes so you could learn the truth. Someone who is that focused on the truth, no matter if learning the full story hurts her or not, is not someone who would bend the truth for her own ends.''

"So you know Paul was exaggerating when he said that."

"Or indulging in wishful thinking."

"You think?"

"I indulge in the same wishful thinking."

She caught her breath. "I don't understand."

He stood and walked to the French doors, looking over the garden. "I feel as nervous as a kid on a first date." Turning, he looked at her. She'd swivelled around on the office chair, not taking her eyes from him.

"I wish you were my fiancée, and then my wife," he said.

Rachel jumped to her feet and flew to him, wrapping her arms around his neck. "That can be arranged. Oh, Luis, I thought you were never going to listen to me. That I would never see you again."

He caught her tightly. "Will you marry me, Rachel? Stay here in Spain and fill my nights with love and my days with delight—as you've done this past week?"

"Yes, yes. Of course." She kissed him, delighting in the feel of his arms around her, of his mouth on hers in the familiar dance of passion. Her blood rushed through her like a tidal wave. He wanted her to marry him. They would not make the mistakes of their parents. She had to tell him about her father and his long ago wish to keep her safe. She would never agree with his method of handling things, but they had taken that first step toward reconciliation. Would he rejoice in her new-found happiness? She believed he would.

"I love you, *querido.* Never leave me," Luis mumbled as he kissed her cheeks, her jaw, her ear.

"I love you. I have forever it seems. I was so happy last week and so devastated when you ordered me away. I thought you only wanted an affair, then I thought maybe you were growing to like me more, and then to have you tell me to leave—"

"I started out wanting an affair. But somewhere along the way, it changed. I want more, now. I want it all. I won't ever tell you to leave again," he said, kissing her.

"I am going now to the village," Esperenza said from the doorway. "But I think you no longer need a ride."

They broke apart to look at Esperenza.

"Congratulations are in order, Esperenza. Rachel has agreed to become my wife," Luis said proudly.

The older woman smiled warmly. "To be sure, I wondered if you'd come to your senses in time, Luis. *Gracias a Dios* you have. I am happy for you, Señor. And for you, Señorita. He's waited a long time for the right person to complete his life."

"She is the right person. For now and for all time," Luis affirmed, kissing her palm.

Rachel basked in the glow of love that filled her. Despite the past, Luis reached out to her, coming for her even before he'd known the truth. She reached up for his kiss as she vowed in her heart to love and honor this man forever.

EPILOGUE

"I'M SO NERVOUS," Rachel said as Luis stopped the car near the curb. The sprawling ranch-style house was situated in a nice suburb of Dallas. The lawn was freshly cut, the edges trimmed. Three cars crowded the driveway.

"If you want to postpone it, we can call and reschedule," he said.

"No. It's all been arranged. How awful to turn back at this juncture." She reached for his hand. "You'll be there with me, right? No matter what she says?"

"*Querido,* we made this appointment over the phone. She is expecting you and is anxious to meet you. It's not like you are going into this cold. Or that she will reject you. You know how much she's longed to see you. Only her commitment to honor the agreement she and your father made so long ago kept her away."

"But she's never seen me. What if she doesn't like me?"

"She will love you. Almost as much as I love you." He raised their linked hands and kissed hers gently.

She squeezed his hand, his words a balm. It really didn't matter if her mother wanted her in her life. She had Luis. It was more than enough.

"Okay." She took a deep breath. "I'm ready."

They walked up to the front door hand-in-hand. She reached out tentatively to ring the bell. For a moment she remembered the bell at the *castillo* she'd rung so many weeks ago. Look how that had turned out. She smiled at her husband of one week, and took another breath. Not many men would spend their honeymoon making an initial visit to strangers. She heard footsteps inside.

The door opened.

A mother's radiant love enveloped her as the woman who looked like an older version of Rachel reached out.

“Oh, my baby, my precious, precious baby. I have missed you so much,” she said, drawing Rachel into her arms and hugging her tightly. Tears ran down her cheeks, and she clung as if she'd never let go.

Rachel let the love wash through her. It would all turn out right. They had all the time now for explanations, for meeting her brothers and sister, and for them to meet Luis. The first step had been the hardest, and it was over.

Her mother pulled back and began to dab her eyes with a tissue, “Come in, come in. My husband and family are so anxious to meet you. And I want to hear every detail of your life since I left. I have missed you every single day.”

Rachel smiled at Luis as they stepped into the house.

“I have it all, now, don't I?” she said for him alone. “Love beyond what I ever dreamed.”

“*Si, mi tresor.*” He reached out to link her hand with his. Together they shared all the love they needed until the end of time.